Lion

FLAMES

Karlene retched as the smoke got into her throat. Coughing himself, Mark led her away from the blaze. For a few minutes, they could do nothing but wait and watch. After what seemed like a lifetime to the waiting crowd, the inferno seemed finally under control. There was a loud hissing noise and two firemen with breathing apparatus were checking to see if it was safe to go into the building.

A new sound cut through the pandemonium. It was the high-pitched scream of a girl, who was racing along the street towards them.

'No!" she shrieked. 'Not *our* house!'

FLAMES

KEITH MILES

Lions
*An imprint of HarperCollins**Publishers***

First published in Great Britain 1995 in Lions
an imprint of HarperCollins Publishers Ltd
77-85 Fulham Palace Road, Hammersmith,
London W6 8JB

The author asserts the moral right to be identified
as the author of this work.

ISBN 0 00 675092 3

Set in Stemple Garamond
Printed and bound in Great Britain by
HarperCollins Manufacturing, Glasgow

Conditions of sale

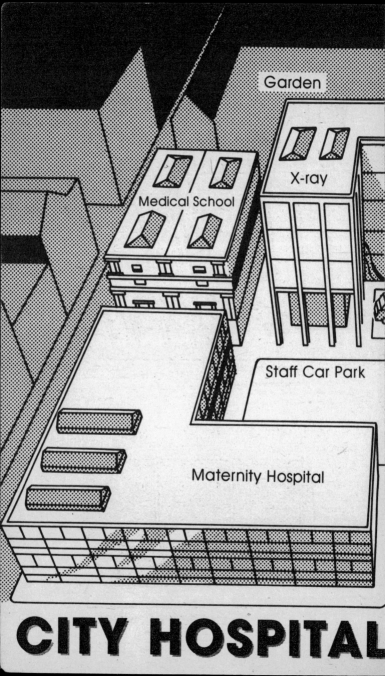

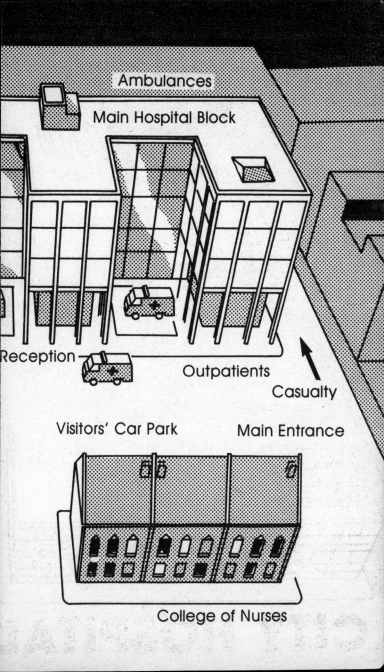

—⌁——CHAPTER ONE—⌁—

The ambulance killed their discussion stone dead. Mark Andrews and Karlene Smith had just come out of the cinema when they heard the wail of the siren. They turned to see the flashing blue lights heading towards them out of the darkness. The vehicle was travelling at top speed.

'Must be an emergency,' said Mark.

'It's a fire,' said Karlene. 'Listen!'

A louder and even more penetrating sound could be heard. The fire engine came roaring into sight, blazing with light and sweeping other traffic aside with its urgency. Its siren was deafening as it swept past.

Karlene saw the ambulance slowing to make a turn.

'Look!' she said in alarm. 'Cameron Street!'

'Do you know someone who lives there?'

'Yes. Janie, Janie Palmer.'

'I hope this is nothing to do with her.'

'So do I, Mark.' She broke into a run. 'Come on!'

Mark was keen to keep pace with her - Karlene's fear was matched by his intense curiosity. He always wanted to be where the action was. They watched the fire engine swing into Cameron Street after the ambulance. As they got nearer, they could see smoke billowing above the houses in the moonlight. The sight of it made Karlene sprint even faster - Mark had a job to keep up with her.

They reached the corner and stopped in their tracks. At the far end of the street was a scene of total confusion. The ambulance and the fire engine had pulled up beside the police car. People milled around wildly in front of the burning house. Flames were coming from the downstairs windows and the column of smoke was thickening all the time. Men were shouting instructions, women were screaming, children were crying.

Karlene was horrified by what she saw.

'Oh, no!' she gulped. 'It *is* Janie's house!'

'Maybe they're not at home,' said Mark, reassuringly.

'They won't stand a chance if they are. Look at those flames. They'll be burnt alive!'

Her heart beating wildly and panic rising, Karlene ran towards the inferno with Mark at her heels. The closer they got, the worse the situation looked. The end-of-terrace house was aflame - fire spurting and crackling and the front door a vivid red rectangle. Mark and Karlene felt the intense heat.

The police were trying to keep the crowd back so that the firemen could uncoil their hoses. The paramedics from the ambulance were already attending to the casualties. There was a gasp of disbelief as a big, sturdy man forced his way through the crowd to the house, a ladder over his shoulder. He placed it against the sill of an upstairs window. One of the fireman tried to stop him.

'You can't go in there, sir!' he warned.

'Get back!' shouted the man.

Kicking the fireman away, he scrambled up the ladder. Smoke was pouring out of the window but he dived recklessly through it. Friends were begging him to come back.

Karlene recognised him at once.

'It's Mr Palmer,' she said, panting. 'Janie's father.'

'He's mad to go back in there.'

'He must be trying to rescue someone.'

'No chance!'

'Please don't let it be Janie! Please, *please!*'

The crew of the fire engine worked swiftly. They turned on their hoses and let the powerful jets of water play on the source of the blaze. It was vital to stop the fire from spreading. The next-door neighbours had already fled their house in terror.

A second ambulance arrived at the scene with two more police cars in support. Uniformed officers tried to impose some order on the chaos; tried to calm people. A woman was already being lifted into the ambulance on a stretcher. Karlene's stomach heaved violently.

'It's Mrs Palmer,' she said.' Janie's mother.'

'There's someone else injured, over there,' said Mark, standing on his toes in order to see. 'Looks like a boy.'

Karlene pushed her way through the crowd to get to the pavement. A young boy was being examined with great care by a paramedic. His clothes were still smouldering. In the unnatural glare, they could see his face was badly burnt. Karlene recoiled as if she'd been hit.

'It's Janie's brother!' she choked.

'Poor kid!'

'Vance... he's only ten. Mark, look at the state of him!'

Paramedics from the other ambulance were helping to lift him gently on to a stretcher. He seemed to be in a far worse condition than his mother. Karlene felt devastated that she could do nothing to help.

'Who else lives in the house?' said Mark.

'Only Janie.'

Karlene was shaking with fear. If her friend was still in the house, she had no hope of coming out alive. Karlene felt weak and staggered slightly. Mark put a steadying arm around her.

'Take it easy,' he soothed.

'Janie's one of my best friends at the club. If anything's happened to her...'

As if to give echo to her thoughts, a groan of despair went up from the onlookers. The ladder against the house was on fire. Flames bit hungrily through its rungs until it crumbled to pieces. There was no sign of Mr Palmer. The window which he'd plunged through was belching acrid smoke.

The noise was ear-splitting; flames crackled, water surged and voices were raised on all sides. More and more people were running to see what was happening. The police struggled to hold them back. Screaming for his father, Vance Palmer was carried into the second ambulance on a stretcher.

Karlene retched as the smoke got into her throat. Coughing himself, Mark led her away from the blaze. For a few minutes, they could do nothing but wait and watch. After what seemed like a lifetime to the waiting crowd, the inferno seemed finally under control. There was a loud hissing noise and two firemen with breathing apparatus were checking to see if it was safe to go into the building.

A new sound cut through the pandemonium. It was the high-pitched scream of a girl, who was racing along the street towards them.

'No!' she shrieked. 'Not *our* house!'

'It's Janie!' said Karlene with relief. 'Thank God!'

'Mum!' wailed the girl. 'Dad! Vance!'

Janie Palmer dashed towards her home but a policeman intercepted her with gentle firmness. He led her slowly back to the gaping group. Neighbours tried to console her. Karlene and Mark elbowed their way through the crowd. When Janie saw her friend, she flung herself into Karlene's arms.

'What happened?' she cried.

'We don't know, Janie.'

'Is anybody hurt? My parents? Vance?'

'They're about to be taken to hospital.'

'Hospital!' Janie was near hysteria. 'Are they that bad?'

Karlene looked at Mark. They were both

thinking the same thing. They just couldn't tell Janie about her father - it would destroy her. She was already reeling from the shock of finding her house in flames. It was better to get her away from the scene altogether. Karlene acted on instinct.

One ambulance had already left. The other was about to move off through the crowd.

'Stop it, Mark,' she said.

'Right!' He ran to flag it down.

Karlene tightened her grip on the distraught Janie.

'Off we go, Janie. I'll come with you.'

'This is terrible, Karlene! Look at our house!'

'I know but there's nothing we can do here,' she said gently.

When Mark had explained to the driver, Karlene and Janie were allowed into the rear of the ambulance. It was the one carrying her mother and Janie trembled at the sight of her mum with an oxygen mask over her mouth. Karlene glanced at Mark apologetically but he waved her away. She was doing the only thing possible.

As the ambulance moved off, Mark turned to look at the house once more. It was a smoking ruin. The door had been burnt off, the windows blown out and the roof had collapsed. Mark felt a surge of sympathy for the Palmer family.

But there was worse to come. Two firemen with breathing apparatus had gone into the house. When they reappeared, they were carrying the motionless figure of Mr Palmer. His clothes were singed, his hands and face were covered in ugly burns.

Clutched in his arms was the animal he'd risked his life to save. It was a tiny puppy. They had died together.

CHAPTER TWO

The journey in the ambulance was an ordeal. Five people were crammed into the back of it with all the equipment. Karlene Smith admired the two paramedics - one of them gave oxygen to Mrs Palmer, the other, a young woman, comforted Janie with soft words of reassurance. But she was still clearly under great stress. She just could not take it all in.

Karlene was worried about the unconscious Mrs Palmer. She was very fond of her and she'd always been kind to Karlene. But her main concern was for Janie who was in a state of deep shock. Her friend, normally so bright and attractive, her long black hair held back in a silver clasp, was shaking violently. Karlene kept her arm around her.

'Wake up, Mum!' pleaded Janie. 'What's wrong with you?'

'Smoke inhalation,' said the man, administering oxygen.

'Is she going to be all right?'

'Calm down, Janie,' soothed Karlene.

'But just look at her!'

'We'll soon be at the hospital.'

Janie turned to Karlene, who hugged her even closer. She kept the girl's face away from her mother so that the sight of the burns didn't distress her even more. Karlene tried to contain her own feelings of horror in order to support her friend.

'What happened to Vance?' asked Janie.

'He went off in the other ambulance.'

'How did the fire start?'

'We've no idea,' said Karlene.

'But I want to know,' said Janie. 'Something must have started it.' She looked down at her mother. 'Tell me, Mum. What was it? What set it of in the first place?'

But her mother was still unconscious. When the paramedic lifted the oxygen mask for a moment, no words came from the blistered lips. Mrs Palmer was beyond their reach.

Janie broke down, sobbing with despair.

'I should've been there. I should've been at home.'

'Don't worry about that now,' said Karlene.

'But I might have been able to help.'

'You don't know that.'

'I might've been able to save Mum and Vance.' She grabbed at her friend. 'I *said* I'd be back, Karlene. Dad made me promise. He'll kill me for this!'

The ambulance swept up to Casualty. Alerted in advance, a team from the Burns Unit was waiting to take over. As the rear doors were opened, the victim was carried out. Mrs Palmer was taken swiftly into the building on her stretcher with a doctor and nurses in attendance.

Karlene was alone in the ambulance with Janie who was still crying piteously. She glanced around dazed and anxious.

'Where *is* Dad?' she grabbed her friend's arm.

'He'll be...along soon, Janie.'

'Was he hurt in the fire? Was he burned?'

'Let's go inside.'

'Tell me the truth, Karlene! Where's my father?'

'I really don't know, Janie.'

'He's not still in the house, is he?'

The very idea produced a fresh burst of sobbing. Janie was inconsolable. Karlene took a firm grip and helped her up from the seat. Shaken herself by what had happened, she tried to put her own emotions aside. She couldn't let her friend down in such a dreadful crisis. Karlene just had to find strength enough to cope.

'Come on, Janie,' she said, gently. 'I've got you.'

———————————⋀———————————

'I can't answer this!' said Bella Denton, staring at the book. 'I can't even *begin* to answer it.'

'What's the question?' asked Gordy Robbins.

'It's from an old RGN paper.'

'Read it out,' he said with a lordly wave. 'Let Doctor Robbins give you his medical opinion.'

'Brace yourself, Gordy. Here it comes. "Mr John Foot, aged thirty-six, sustained a head injury when he fell from a ladder while cleaning windows. He is now in the trauma ward and is unconscious." Surprise, surprise!'

'Get to the question, Bel.'

'Right. "Identify Mr Reid's likely problems

while he is unconscious and describe the observations a nurse should make, including their significance." Over to you.'

'I know what my first observation would be.'

'What's that?'

'Give up window-cleaning.'

'The man's unconscious,' said Suzie Hembrow, coming in from the kitchen with a cup of coffee. 'You're asked what his likely problems are.'

'Bad dreams,' said Gordy.

'Gordy!' snorted Bella.

'He's having nightmares about all those dirty windows.'

'You're hopeless!'

'We haven't done head cases yet, Bel.'

'You *are* a head case!'

Gordy was defensive. 'I'm only a first-year. I don't know everything. Besides,' he said, 'they can't expect you to answer difficult questions like that when you've only been a student nurse for five minutes.'

'You're right,' said Bella, tossing the book aside. 'I shouldn't torment myself by looking at old exam papers. I'm not ready yet.'

The three of them were relaxing in the house they shared with Karlene and Mark. All five of them were studying at the hospital. Mark and Bella were student nurses, Suzie a student radiographer and Karlene was studying physiotherapy.

Gordy was at medical school; sometimes he felt

this gave him additional charisma - the fact that he would become a doctor.

'One day, Bel,' he said, airily, 'you may be lucky enough to work with me at some hospital.'

'Don't be so pompous,' chided Suzie. '*You'd* be lucky to have Bella working alongside you.'

'Yes!' agreed Bella. 'Nurses are just as important as doctors. You get paid more, that's all.'

'We get paid more because we make the big decisions.'

'Like deciding which nurse to pounce on next!'

'That's rich, coming from you, Bel!' he retorted. 'You pounce on every man in a white coat in the hospital.'

'No, I don't!'

'They all walk around in pairs for safety.'

'Gordy!'

'He's only teasing you,' said Suzie with a smile. 'Gordy knows quite well that you're very selective when it comes to boyfriends.'

'That's why I'd never select *him* !'

'Thank God for that!' he said with a grin.

She grabbed the book again and hurled it at him, scoring a direct hit on the side of his head. Gordy howled in pain and started to throw it back.

'Don't, Gordy. It's not my book. It belongs to Mark.'

'You slung it at me.'

'Only because you asked for it.'

Suzie snatched the book from him and put it aside.

'Now, now, children, the fight's over.' she said, pleasantly.

They heard the scrape of a key in the lock and the front door opening and shutting. Mark came into the room. His face was ashen, his shoulders drooped. Gordy noticed how dejected he seemed.

'It must have been a dreadful film,' he said.

Mark blinked. 'Film? Oh, I'd forgotten that. The fire put it right out of my mind.'

'*Fire*?' said Suzie, sitting up in alarm.

'In Cameron Street. That friend of Karlene's - Janie Palmer. Her house burnt down. It was terrifying.'

'Where's Karlene?' said Bella, suddenly anxious.

'Gone to the hospital with Janie.'

'Was Janie hurt?' said Suzie.

'No. She was lucky. She wasn't at home.'

'What about the others?' asked Suzie.

Mark sighed. 'Mrs Palmer and her son were badly injured. They were rushed to hospital. Karlene and Janie went in the ambulance with Janie's mum.'

'How dreadful!' said Bella. 'They're such a lovely family. I've met them a couple of times.'

Suzie could see the grief in Mark's eyes.

'What about *Mr* Palmer?' she said, quietly.

Mark's lip trembled. 'He's...he's dead, Suzie... he died in the blaze.'

Bella was stunned. 'Mr Palmer? *Dead?* He can't be. I mean...I saw him only last week. He's such a nice man.'

'A brave one, too,' said Mark.

'Do they know what caused the fire?' said Gordy.

'Not yet. It's too soon to say. But I did overhear one of the coppers at the scene. He suggested a possible cause.'

'What did he say, Mark?'

'Arson.'

They sat in the waiting room for over an hour. Janie's cup of coffee lay untouched on the table in front of her. She brooded in silence. Her face was full of pain and guilt. Her hands were clasped tightly together. Karlene watched her with growing concern. Her friend seemed to be going through some kind of private torture.

Janie came out of her reverie and turned to Karlene.

'I knew something like this would happen,' she said.

'Why?' asked Karlene.

'It's my punishment.'

'For what, Janie?'

'For breaking my promise. Dad will go up the wall.'

'Tell me about your promise.'

'I just couldn't help it, Karlene. I had to stay.'

'Stay where, Janie?'

'At the club.'

'Is that where you were tonight? The Caribbean Club?'

Janie nodded. 'I was supposed to be home at ten.'

'So? You were a little late. You were having fun.'

Her friend bit her lip and fought off fresh tears. 'There was more to it than that, Karlene.'

'What happened, Janie?'

The question hung in the air. Karlene waited for an answer that never came - Janie had said enough. She fell silent again, wrestling with her conscience.

A nurse walked towards them. She was a trim Chinese woman in a smart blue uniform. Janie and Karlene stood up expectantly. The nurse's neutral expression told them nothing.

'Please,' said Janie, anxiously. 'How are they?'

'Well, your mother has improved slightly,' said the nurse.

'Can I see her? Can I talk to Mum?'

'I'm afraid not. The doctor has given her a sedative. She needs her sleep. You may be able to see her tomorrow.'

'Tomorrow! Why not now?' protested Janie. 'She's my mother.'

'The doctor knows best,' said Karlene, trying to soothe her friend.

'What about Vance? Can I see *him*?'

'I'm afraid not,' said the nurse, gently. 'His

condition is more critical. The doctor has only just finished with him.'

'How bad is he?'

'Your brother is very poorly. The doctor will explain to you in detail. I've come to take you to his office.' She turned to Karlene. 'Did you ring her uncle?'

'He should be here any moment,' said Karlene.

'I don't want my uncle,' complained Janie. 'I want to see Mum and Vance. I want to see Dad as well. Where is he? What have you done with him?'

'The doctor will tell you all you need to know.'

'You're hiding something from me!'

'Come with me, please, Janie.'

'Do as she says,' urged Karlene. 'I'll wait here for you.'

'But I want you with me, Karlene.'

'Your friend can join you in a moment,' said the nurse.

'Why?' demanded Janie. 'Why are you taking me off on my own? What's the doctor going to tell me that Karlene can't hear? I need her there with me.'

Karlene saw the look on the nurse's face and understood. It was like a hard punch in the pit of her stomach. She was stunned for a moment. Then she fought to control her own shock.

'Do as they ask, Janie,' she said. 'I'll be right here.'

Karlene's face couldn't hide what she felt. Janie realised the awful truth - her father must be dead.

She swayed and had to be steadied by them both. Janie was stricken with grief. All her vitality drained away. She didn't even have the strength to cry. When she had recovered from the initial shock, she let herself be led away gently by the nurse.

Karlene's heart went out to her friend. Janie had been rocked by a whole succession of cruel blows. Karlene herself was finding it difficult to accept that Mr Palmer was dead. She remembered him climbing the ladder to get back into the house. He'd always made her feel welcome when she went there. It was so sad to think she'd never see him again.

But Janie's loss was far greater and she would never be able to cope with it on her own. Janie needed a friend badly now. It was going to be a long night.

CHAPTER THREE

Next morning, Gordy Robbins and Mark Andrews walked to the hospital together. It was a fine but chilly day. Gordy wore his garish wool jacket and green chinos. In his old denim jacket, Mark looked rather dowdy beside his friend.

As he caught sight of the building, Mark thought of the fire and the appalling damage it had left behind. He wondered how Mrs Palmer and her son were doing in the Burns Unit. Mr Palmer, he knew, would be lying in the hospital morgue.

Gordy's mind was on something else.

'Do you think she'll come round in the end, Mark?'

'Who?'

'Suzie. She can't hold me off for ever. I'm sure she fancies me on the quiet.'

'Suzie just doesn't want to get involved.'

'That's what's so frustrating!' said Gordy. 'I share the house with this gorgeous girl and she keeps me at arm's length.'

'Maybe you're not her type,' said Mark, tactfully.

'I'll wear down her resistance in time.'

'Don't bank on it, Gordy.'

'I drive most girls crazy. Why not Suzie?'

Mark said nothing. He pushed his glasses up the bridge of his nose. Still rather shy with girls himself, he didn't feel able to offer any advice.

Gordy was much more experienced. Or, at least, he pretended to be.

'It's this stupid rule of Suzie's,' said Gordy. 'Because we share a house, we mustn't get involved.'

'Nothing stupid about that,' said Mark. 'If two of us become an item, it makes it hard on the other three. Forget Suzie. Find someone else.'

'Only as a stop-gap,' said Gordy. 'I'll still carry a torch for Suzie. She'll always be top of my list.'

'I think Suzie's got that message by now.'

Gordy went through the main gate of the hospital with his jaunty stride. His face was beaming. He was in good spirits. He sensed that he would have an enjoyable day at the medical school.

A female voice shattered the illusion.

'Gordy!'

He stopped dead and stiffened, Mark beside him.

A tall, slim, shapely girl was running towards them. Her fair hair swinging, her pretty features glowing.

'Hi, Gordy!' she said.

'Harriet!'

'I was hoping I'd bump into you.'

'Er, yes,' gulped Gordy. 'Nice to see you again.'

'Aren't you going to introduce me?' she prompted.

'What? Oh, sorry...This is Mark Andrews.'

'Hi, Mark,' she said, shaking hands with him. 'I'm Harriet Collins. An old and very special friend of Gordy's.'

Gordy looked more uncomfortable than ever.

'Nice to meet you, Harriet,' said Mark. 'You'll have to excuse me, I'm afraid. I mustn't be late.'

'Don't leave us!' begged Gordy.

'I have to,' he said, amused by the look of panic on Gordy's face. 'You two must have a lot to catch up on. I'd only be in the way.'

'Wait!' Gordy clutched at him but Mark walked away across the car park. Harriet stared up at Gordy, her eyes shining. She let out a sigh of sheer pleasure.

'You look wonderful!' she said.

'Thanks, Harriet...Er, so do you.'

'Are you pleased to see me?'

'Yes, yes,' he lied, searching for an escape.

'I wanted to surprise you.'

'Well, you certainly did that!'

'It's brilliant just to *be* with you again, Gordy.'

'Is it? Good.' He glanced at his watch. 'Heavens! Look at the time. I must be off.'

'Of course.'

He backed slowly away. 'Nice to...meet you again.'

'I just had to get in touch with you.'

'I'm glad you did,' he said, uneasily.

'That's why I moved down here.'

Gordy froze. 'What do you mean?'

'To be near you,' she said, touching his arm. 'You're going to be seeing a lot of me from now on, Gordy.'

'I am?'

'Yes, I've taken a job at the hospital!'

'*Here!*'

'As a receptionist.'

'Oh...great...'

Gordy was in the grip of cold terror. His mouth went dry and his eyes misted over. He couldn't move a muscle.

Harriet kissed him softly on the cheek.

'I knew you'd be thrilled,' she whispered.

'What time did you get to bed, Karlene?' asked Bella.

'Three o'clock.'

'I'm amazed you made it to the hospital this morning.'

'So am I,' said Karlene. 'I'd have been better off staying here and sleeping in the waiting room.'

'I bet Janie was glad to have you by her side.'

'She was, Bella. When she saw the fire, she went to pieces. You know, it's strange, for some reason Janie keeps saying *she* was responsible. She blames herself for her father's death.'

'That's crazy. It must be the shock that's making her say that.'

'I know. She wasn't even there.'

They were having lunch in the hospital canteen. Noise was reverberating around the room. Karlene found herself shrinking from the continual clatter - she was so exhausted and anxious, she found the noise almost unbearable.

'How do you feel?' said Bella.

'Shattered. It was a nightmare."

'Any news from the Burns Unit?'

'Yes,' said Karlene. 'Mrs Palmer's much better today. She only suffered first-degree burns. They look hideous and must be incredibly painful but they should heal up of their own accord.'

'What about Vance?'

'He's far worse.'

'Third-degree burns?'

'I'm afraid so, Bella. They completely destroy all the skin layers, including the sweat glands and hair follicles.'

'It sounds really dreadful!'

'It is,' said Karlene. 'I couldn't understand why Vance wasn't screaming with pain. But his nerve ends had been burned as well. He just felt numb.'

'How did he suffer worse injuries than his mother?'

'Because he went back into the burning house.'

Bella gasped. 'He *what*?'

'The fire started downstairs,' explained Karlene. 'Vance was in his bedroom and his mother was in the bath. When she saw the smoke, she threw on her dressing gown and rushed to grab her son. They escaped as the fire was getting a real hold.'

'So why did Vance go back into the house?'

'For Coco...His puppy.'

'Where was he?'

'He was supposed to be in his kennel in the garden but Vance had smuggled him up to his room. That's why he had to go back into the flames.'

'Where was Mr Palmer all this time?'

'Out looking for Janie, apparently,' said Karlene. 'I still haven't worked out why. Anyway, when he got back to the house, it was like a raging inferno. Vance came staggering out in tears, begging him to rescue Coco.'

'So that's why he went up the ladder.'

'They could hear the dog barking frantically. Mr Palmer was determined to save him. Instead of that...'

There was a long silence. Bella grew introspective.

'Who broke the news to Janie?'

'The doctor.'

'How did she take it?'

'She's completely stunned.'

'I'm not surprised,' said Bella, quietly. 'I was in a daze for weeks when my father died. And that was expected. I mean, he'd been ill for a long time and we had plenty of warning. Not Janie. It fell on top of her like a ton of bricks. I feel really sorry for her. Where is she now?'

'Staying with her uncle and aunt, said Karlene.'

'Have you met them?'

'Yes, they came to the hospital last night to fetch Janie. They only live a few miles away.'

'At least she's got someone to look after her.'

'Only one problem - Janie doesn't get on with them. She never has.'

'Why not?'

'She wouldn't say,' said Karlene. 'I've only ever seen Janie at the club or back at her house. She's always full of life and ready for a laugh.' She moved stiffly in her seat, exhausted from the night's drama. 'But there's another side to her. She's hiding something, Bella.'

Mark came up with a plate of food.

'Mind if I join you?' he asked.

'Of course not,' said Bella. 'Take a seat.'

'Thanks,' said Mark, settling down beside them. 'Have you heard about Gordy?'

'What's he been up to now?' said Karlene.

'I know,' added Bella, cynically. 'Chasing another girl around the medical school.'

Mark shook his head. 'Gordy is the prey this time.'

'Who'd be mad enough to chase him!'

'Be fair, Bella,' said Karlene, reasonably. 'Gordy can sometimes look quite attractive. In a certain light.'

'Yes - pitch darkness!'

'Harriet obviously had a real crush on him,' said Mark.

'Who's Harriet?'

'Harriet Collins. I don't know who she is, Bella, but she was waiting to ambush Gordy this morning. She had stars in her eyes but he couldn't get away quick enough.'

The girls laughed at this vision of Gordy on the run.

'I wish I'd been there,' said Bella. 'Who is she?'

'An old flame.'

———⋀———

Suzie was walking around the angle of the main block when she heard the hissing noise. She stopped to look round.

'Over here!' hissed a voice.

'Where are you?'

'Behind the van.'

Suzie saw him at last. Gordy Robbins was tucked in between a delivery van and a wall. He looked furtive.

'What are you hiding in there for?' she asked, amazed.

'I'm not hiding, Suzie,' he said, coming out with great caution. 'I was waiting to walk you home, that's all.'

'Is this some kind of game, Gordy?'

'No, no. I just fancied company.' He contrived a weak smile. 'And you're the best company there is.'

Suzie sighed. 'Now don't start all that again!'

'I'm not trying to chat you up or anything.'

'That's a relief!'

'If you prefer, I won't say a word all the way home.'

'I'll hold you to that, Gordy. Come on.'

Suzie began to walk towards the main gates of

the hospital but he took her by the arm and guided her away.

'Let's go out by the side entrance,' he suggested. 'for a change.'

'But I need to pop into Reception.'

He blanched. 'Do you *have* to, Suzie?'

'Won't take a minute. Come in with me.'

'No thanks,' he said, glancing fearfully at Reception. 'I'll wait out here.'

'Are you afraid of something?'

'Don't be silly. Nothing frightens me.' He grinned. 'Except your tape of Emmylou Harris.'

She gave him a playful push. 'Stay right here.'

Suzie ran across to the main doors and went through into Reception. It was as busy as ever. The girls at the Reception Desk were besieged with enquiries. Suzie didn't even see Harriet who was making an appointment for a patient over the telephone.

She went straight to the little shop on the far side. It sold newspapers, magazines, biscuits, sandwiches and sweets. One of the Hospital Volunteers - a sweet old lady with rimless spectacles - was serving behind the counter. Suzie waited until the shop was clear.

She looked around guiltily then plunged in.

'Can I help you, dear?' said the old lady.

'Have you got any Mars bars, please?' asked Suzie.

'They should be on the top shelf.'

'There's only one left.'

34

'In that case, we'll open another box.'

The old lady knelt down to search for something under the counter. Suzie glanced round nervously. If Gordy had been with her, she would only have bought one Mars bar. On her own, she was overtaken by a stronger urge.

'Here we are, dear.'

The old lady resurfaced with a new box. 'How many would you like?'

'How many are there in the box?'

'A dozen.'

Suzie hesitated - then reached in her bag. 'I'll take them all, please.'

Bella could not resist teasing Gordy. She had been the victim of so many of his practical jokes that she wanted to get her own back. Bella and Mark were the first home from the hospital. She sat in the window until she saw Suzie approaching with Gordy.

Bella dived for the telephone and picked it up.

'Here he comes, Mark!'

'This is cruel.'

'Gordy deserves it.'

'What if it doesn't work?'

'It'll work,' she promised. 'Just watch me.'

As the front door opened, Bella put the receiver to her ear and spoke into the mouthpiece. When the others entered the room, she was in full flight.

'Yes, Harriet,' she said. 'Gordy would love that.'

Hearing her words, Gordy backed away as if struck by an invisible fist.

'Harriet! How on earth did she get my number?' he whispered, hoarsely.

'Call round any evening,' invited Bella, warmly.

'No, no!' he croaked.

'He'll cook supper for you.'

'You've got to be joking!'

'Yes, Harriet. Don't worry. We'll make sure the two of you are left alone together.'

'Don't you dare!' howled Gordy.

'Got a pen handy? Here's our address...'

Gordy made a dive for the telephone and seized it.

'Look, you're not to come here, Harriet!' he ordered. 'Do you understand? And please don't ring me again. I've got exams. I'm revising every night. In fact...'

His voice trailed off as he realised that there was nobody at the end of the line. Gordy growled and turned on Bella. He slammed down the receiver.

'Very funny!'

'I was giving you a dose of your own medicine, Doctor Robbins,' laughed Bella. 'Doesn't taste very nice, does it?'

'You nearly gave me a heart attack.'

Suzie was beginning to work out what was happening.

'So that's why you were so strange at the hospital.'

'Gordy's *always* strange,' said Bella.

'He's being pursued by an ex,' explained Mark.

'Yes,' admitted Gordy, flopping into a chair. 'Harriet Collins. Of all people. I hoped I'd outrun her. She's a menace.'

'What's she doing here?' said Suzie.

'Working at the hospital. In Reception.'

'No wonder you refused to go in there with me.'

'I intend to give Harriet a wide berth.'

'What if she finds out where you live?' taunted Bella.

'Then I'll know who told her, won't I?' he said. 'And I'll come after you with a box of surgical instruments.'

'Harriet seemed like an attractive girl,' said Mark.

Gordy grimaced. 'That's what I thought. Then. I take a very different view of her now. She's lethal.'

'Why?' asked Bella.

'That's a private matter.'

'If you won't tell me, I'll ask Harriet herself.'

'You're sadistic, Bella!'

'I just love dark secrets.'

'Give him a break,' said Suzie, kindly. 'Sounds to me as if Gordy's had enough shocks for one day. Back off.'

'Thanks, Suzie,' he said. 'At least I have one friend.'

'Two,' reminded Bella. 'Suzie, and Harriet Collins.'

'Stop going on about her!'

Bella relented and they began to exchange notes about their respective days at the hospital. They learnt a lot from each other that way.

It was Mark's turn to cook a meal. Suzie drifted into the kitchen after him.

'Don't make anything for me,' she said.

'Why not? Eating out for a change?'

'Can't afford to, Mark. No, I'm just not hungry.'

'It's only a tuna salad. I'll make plenty in case you feel a bit peckish later on.'

'Don't bother about me,' she insisted. 'And you needn't worry about Karlene, either. She'll eat at the hospital. She's meeting Janie Palmer.'

'That means another long vigil.'

'You know Karlene. She never lets her friends down.'

Karlene found her in the waiting room, sitting beside her aunt, a buxom woman in her forties. Janie seemed to be in a dream. Slumped in her chair, she stared ahead of her with glassy eyes. There was an air of defeat about her.

'Hi, Janie,' said Karlene. 'Hello, Mrs Naylor.'

Linda Naylor looked up with a sad smile. Janie rallied slightly and sat up. Her aunt took the opportunity to leave.

'Stay with her, Karlene. I need to find the Ladies.'

'Down that corridor and first right, Mrs Naylor.'

'Thanks.' She got to her feet and spoke in a confidential whisper. 'See if you can help Janie. We could do nothing with her. She cried all night.'

'It must've been a big shock for all of you.'

'It was, Karlene. Especially for my husband. Greg was his brother-in-law. To die in a fire like that! It's heart-breaking! We'll never get over it.'

'No, it must be very hard, Mrs Naylor.'

Karlene sensed that Linda Naylor was more interested in her own grief than in that of her niece. As she left the waiting room, Janie looked resentful.

'Good riddance!' she said, vehemently.

'Janie!'

'She's never liked me, Karlene.'

'That's not true. Your aunt's a very kind woman.'

'You don't know her like I do.'

'Forget about her,' said Karlene. 'How are *you*?'

Janie gave a despairing shrug of the shoulders. 'I feel dreadful.'

'Did you manage to get *any* sleep?'

'None at all.'

'You should ask for a sedative from your GP?'

'I'll be OK.'

'Can I get you anything? Tea, coffee, Pepsi?'

'No thanks.'

Karlene sat beside her. 'What's the latest news?'

'Mum's on the mend. They're talking about letting her come home in a few days.'

'That's wonderful news, Janie!'

'Except there's no home to come back to, is there? It's all gone, Karlene,' she said, bitterly. 'That's what keeps hitting me again and again. No home, no Dad, no nothing!'

'You have got something. Your mum, your brother. Me.'

Janie squeezed her arm. 'You've been great.'

'Lean on me all you want.'

'Do you really mean that?'

'Of course.'

'I know I can trust you. Not like Aunty Linda.'

'Mrs Naylor's probably doing her best for you.'

'I hate staying in her house.'

Karlene patted her hand gently. 'How's Vance?'

'Still on the critical list.'

'What did the doctor say to you?'

'Something about a Rule of Nine. I couldn't understand a word of it. Have you any idea what he was on about?'

'I think so,' said Karlene. 'They mentioned it last night so I looked it up in the library. They calculate the area of burns by using something called Wallace's Rule of Nines.'

'What does that mean?'

'The body is divided up into sections of nine per cent. Each arm is nine per cent. Each leg is twice times nine per cent and so on.'

Janie was mystified. 'What's the point of it all?'

'When they know the extent of the burns, they can see how much treatment is needed. They can also work out how much fluid replacement is required.' Karlene gave a smile of apology. 'Sorry. I don't want to blind you with science.'

'The doctor said Vance had nineteen per cent burns.'

'Then he may be lucky.'

'Lucky!' exclaimed Janie. 'To be scarred for life!'

'At least, he may *have* a life,' said Karlene, gently. 'The young and the old are most at risk from burns. Their resistance is not as strong.' She smiled wryly. 'Oh, dear! There I go again, sounding like a medical textbook.'

'Vance is only ten. He must be terrified.'

'They'll look after him, Janie. I promise you.'

'Why can't *I* speak to him?' said Janie. 'His face is so badly burned, they won't even let me see him.'

'I think it might be the other way around. They won't let Vance see *you*.'

'What do you mean?'

'Because you might upset him, Janie.'

'I'm his sister. How could I possibly upset him?'

'By letting him know just how bad he is,' explained Karlene. 'It was all in that book I read. There are no mirrors in the Burns Unit. People with facial disfigurement are not allowed to look at themselves until the time is right. It could frighten them too much. Can you understand what I'm saying?'

'Not really.'

'*You'd* be Vance's mirror, Janie. He'd only have to see your reaction to know how dreadful his face must look. That would scare him even more.'

'I never thought of that.'

'He may be kept here a very long time, Janie. You must learn to take things day-by-day.'

Janie nodded sadly, then looked up at her.

'I don't want to go back with Aunty Linda tonight.'

'I think you'll have to.'

'Couldn't I stay with you, Karlene?'

'There's no room.'

'I'd sleep anywhere. On a sofa, on a floor.'

'That wouldn't do you any good at all, Janie. You need a proper bed. Besides, you must think of your mum. She'd be really disturbed if you just walked out of your aunt's house like that. So would Mrs Naylor.'

'Who cares about Aunty Linda!' sneered the other.

'Don't you?'

'No. I never have. It's awful being with her.'

'Where else could you have gone?'

'I don't know.'

'And where else could your mum go?' reasoned Karlene. 'When she comes out of hospital, she'll need a lot of care and attention.'

'Yeah, I know.'

'She's going to rely very heavily on you, Janie. Make an effort with your aunt. Your mum won't get much rest if the house is full of tension.'

'It's Aunty Linda's fault. She doesn't like me and this has only made it worse.'

'In what way?'

'She blames me for what happened.'

'But you had nothing to do with the fire, Janie.'

'Yes, I did,' confessed the girl. 'That's why I hate Aunty Linda so much. She's telling the truth. If I hadn't gone off last night, there wouldn't have *been* a fire!'

The chimes of Big Ben boomed out on the television. Mark had switched on to watch *News at Ten*. He was alone in the living room with Suzie. She put aside the magazine she'd been reading and pretended to yawn.

'I'm off to bed,' she announced.

'Bit early for you, isn't it?'

'I'm tired, Mark.'

'Grab the bathroom while you can,' he advised. 'Bella will be back from her date before long and Karlene will want a long soak when she gets home from the hospital.'

'She deserves it.'

They heard footsteps above their head in Gordy's room.

'He's been up there all evening,' she observed. 'Is Gordy actually studying for once?'

'No, Suzie,' he said with a grin. 'He's lying low. Hiding from that old girlfriend of his. I never thought I'd see the day when Gordy ran away from female company.'

They laughed. As Suzie went upstairs she didn't feel at all tired. Once inside her room, she locked the door and crossed to the little wardrobe. She groped around until she found what she wanted.

She sat on the bed with the box on her lap. It was hours since she'd touched any food and she was starving. Opening the box, she took out the first Mars bar and tore off the wrapper. She bit into it, chewing happily.

Suzie fondled the box.

She was going to eat them all.

CHAPTER FIVE

Bella came back to the house just before midnight. She found Karlene in the kitchen, nibbling at the remains of the tuna salad. Karlene looked exhausted.

'How did you get on?' she said, wearily.

Bella pulled a face. 'It was OK, I suppose.'

'Is that all?'

'Afraid so. Neil was a bit of a let-down.'

'I thought you liked him.'

'I did,' said Bella. 'He's the best-looking guy in my year - really good for a laugh. I've always fancied him.'

'So what went wrong?'

'On our own, he was completely different, Karlene. He clammed up on me. I could hardly get a word out of him. I think I'll go back to the gorgeous Dr Damian Holt. At least he knew how to chat me up properly.'

'Damian was a hunk,' agreed Karlene. 'Neil may've been nervous on a first date. He'll be much better next time.'

'There won't *be* a next time.'

'Have you given him the push already?'

'More or less.'

Karlene grinned. 'You're so ruthless, Bella.'

'I expect more action,' she said, airily. 'Neil failed the litmus test - so out he goes.'

'Another boyfriend bites the dust!'

'Forget him,' said Bella. 'He's history. What's the news from the hospital? Did you see Janie?'

'Yes,' said Karlene with a sigh. 'I've only just got back.'

'How is she?'

'Completely shell-shocked.'

'I know the feeling.'

'Janie's lost her father and her home; her mother was injured in the fire and her brother was so badly burned that he may have to stay in hospital for months.' Karlene shook her head. 'It's a hell of a lot to cope with, Bella.'

'It would crush anybody.'

'On top of all that, there's this friction with her aunt and uncle. Janie can't stand living with them.'

'Why not?'

'I still haven't got to the bottom of it,' said Karlene. 'But I know they criticise her a lot. And Mrs Naylor - that's the aunt - has been badgering Janie about the fire. Even claiming that it was Janie's fault.'

'That's rubbish!'

'I told her that.'

'Janie was nowhere near the house when the fire started,' Bella insisted.

'It doesn't stop her blaming herself. She feels she should have been there, Bella. That's why her aunt's gibes hurt so much. Janie says there's a lot of truth in them but she won't explain why.'

Bella looked thoughtful. 'Where *was* Janie last night?' she asked.

'At the Caribbean Club.'

'Are you sure, Karlene?'

'That's what she told me.'

'But do you think she could've been lying?'

'Why should she?'

'I was just remembering what you told me about her father. That when the fire started, he was out looking for Janie.'

'That's right.'

'Then surely the first place he'd go to would be the club. It's not all that far from the house. If Janie was there, why didn't Mr Palmer find her?'

'Good question.'

'Try putting it to Janie.'

'No, Bella,' decided Karlene. 'I'm her friend. I don't want to lose her trust. And I'd certainly do that if I start to put any pressure on her. Janie will tell me what she wants to in her own time. On the other hand...'

'Yes?'

'There's nothing to stop you making a few discreet enquiries.'

'Count me in, if you need help.'

'Thanks, Bella. I may do that.' She smiled. 'In fact, you can start helping me right this minute - get me out of this chair and carry me upstairs. I haven't got the strength to move.'

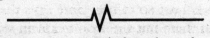

The nightmare was so terrifyingly real.

Wearing his pyjamas, Vance Palmer was playing

in his bedroom with Coco. He rolled a ball across the floor and the puppy scampered after it. Coco tapped the ball with a paw and it rolled on. He yapped excitedly.

'Be quiet, Coco!' hissed the boy. 'You know you're not allowed up here. Dad will go bananas if he finds out.' He cradled the dog lovingly in his arms and it stopped yapping. 'There's a good dog! If you keep quiet you can stay the whole night. OK?'

'Vance! Vance!'

His mother was yelling from the bathroom.

'Vance! Quick! Get out!'

He heard her running along the landing. Grabbing Coco, he tossed him into a cupboard and shut the door. He was terrified that his mother would see the dog.

The door of his room was flung open and Mrs Palmer ran in. She was wearing only a dressing gown. Vance could smell something burning. Smoke drifted into the bedroom. His mother caught hold of him.

'Come on!' she shrieked. 'We've got to get out!'

'What's happened?'

'The house is on fire!'

'Fire!' He was horrified. 'But I'm not dressed, Mum.'

'It doesn't matter! Come on!'

He snatched his dressing gown from the back of the door, threw it around his shoulders then went downstairs with her. Flames were coming from the kitchen and smoke was everywhere. They both retched. Mrs Palmer was a big woman. Vance felt her hold him tight to her - she used her body to shield him from the worst of the blaze.

All that Vance could think about was Coco.

'Wait, Mum!' he shouted. 'I've got to go back.'

But his mother didn't even hear him above the crackle of the fire. Escape was her priority. She half-carried him across the hall. His protests grew louder and louder.

'Let me go back, Mum! Let me go back! Please!'

When they got to the front door, they seemed to be engulfed in smoke. Mrs Palmer almost keeled over. With the last of her strength, she wrenched it open and hauled her son outside.

Vance saw their neighbours rushing to help. He was bewildered by the sea of faces. Mrs Palmer staggered clear of the house and then collapsed into the arms of some friends. Vance looked back at his home. One fear dominated his mind.

His puppy was trapped upstairs in the cupboard.

'Hold on, Coco!' he screamed. 'I'll get you out!'

Vance darted back into the house without a thought for his own safety. He was too late. The fire had spread everywhere.

'I'm coming, Coco. I'm coming for you.' Vance ran straight into a sheet of flame. His whole body seemed to be on fire. The pain was unbearable. 'Wait there, Coco! I'll save you!'

He cried out in agony and woke himself up with a start.

'It's all right, Vance,' soothed the nurse, easing him gently back on to the bed. 'Go back to sleep.'

The boy blinked. He was lying in a darkened room. His body was stiff and aching. His face felt sore, puffy and bruised. His eyelids seemed to be partly stitched down. When he tried to speak, his lips were too swollen to let any words pass through them.

Vance moved his arm and felt a sharp twinge. There was a tube sticking into his vein. What were they doing to him? He just couldn't get his bearings at all.

'Where are Mum and Dad?' he thought. 'Where's Janie?'

He had a horrible feeling of being held prisoner.

They had taken away his best friend in the whole world.

'Coco!' he said to himself. 'Where *are* you?'

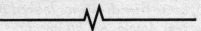

Mark was amazed when he came into the kitchen that morning. Gordy was just finishing his breakfast.

'What's got you up so early, Gordy?' he said.

'I wanted to be first in the bathroom for a change.'

'It *is* a change. You're usually the last.'

Gordy spread marmalade on to a piece of toast then popped it in his mouth. Mark was surprised again.

'I thought you didn't like marmalade.'

'I don't,' said Gordy, 'but this is all that was left.'

'What about that apricot jam you bought?'

'Vanished.'

'It can't have,' said Mark, going to the cupboard. 'I saw it there only last night. A big jar. Almost full.'

'It's not there now.'

Mark opened the cupboard and searched it carefully.

'You're right. That's funny. Wherever did it go?'

'I'll leave you to work that one out, Mark,' said Gordy as he got up from the table. 'While you're solving the case of the Missing Jam Jar, I'll be on my way.'

'But you'll get there an hour before time.'

'That's the idea.' Gordy waved his farewell. 'Say bye-bye to the girls for me. See you later.'

He let himself out of the house and walked briskly along the street. The hospital was a comfortable stroll away but Gordy didn't take the usual route. Instead of heading for the main entrance, he chose a side-road which led him around the perimeter of the site. Though it put an extra five or six minutes on the journey, he didn't mind. It was worth it.

It enabled him to get to the medical school without having to walk past the main hospital block. After the ambush on the previous day, he was taking no chances. Arriving very early by a different route would fool her.

'Good morning, Gordy!'

'Harriet!' he gasped.

'I was hoping to catch you before I start work.'

His plot had failed. When he came through the entrance hall of the medical school, Harriet was waiting for him. She looked at him with simpering affection. Gordy broke out in a cold sweat.

'I just had to see you,' she said.

'Did you?'

'We didn't have time to talk properly yesterday.'

'I'm really busy today as well.'

'That's why I wanted to catch you. To make a date - to pick up where we left off.'

'Now, listen, Harriet...'

'What's the best time for you?'

'There *isn't* a best time.'

'I'm free every evening. Just name the day.'

'I can't, I'm afraid. I've left my diary at home.'

'OK,' she said, easily. 'Give me a ring when you get back this evening. Better still, let me call you. What's your phone number?'

Gordy remembered the joke Bella had played on him and the last thing he wanted to do was to let Harriet have his number. It would be a foot in the door for her. That would be disastrous.

'The phone's out of order,' he lied.

'Ring me from a call box, then,' she suggested. Harriet gave him a slip of paper. 'Here's my address. It's only a bedsit but I have use of the phone. The number's at the bottom.'

I've got to get rid of her! he told himself. I've got to end this once and for all. Be brutal, Gordy. Go for the jugular. It's the only way.

He took a deep breath...but the wrong words came out.

'You look very smart this morning, Harriet.' He looked flustered.

'Thank you,' she said, basking in the compliment. 'You look as handsome as ever, Gordy. I'm sure you'll be a great doctor.'

'That's not what my tutor thinks!' he said, ruefully.

'You have such an air of quiet authority. That's what first turned me on,' she told him, stroking his arm. 'Your authority - and your sexy legs! What was it about me that turned *you* on?'

Gordy couldn't remember. What leapt into his mind were all the things about Harriet that had scared him off. She was too keen, for one thing. And here she was, behaving the same again.

'What was it, Gordy?' she demanded. 'Tell me.'

'Er...maybe this isn't the time and place,' he said.

'Save it until we're alone, then.'

'That may not be for a long time, Harriet,' he said as he stalled. 'I'm tied up for weeks on end. They work us really hard in medical school.'

'That's all right,' she said, sweetly. 'I'm very patient. After all, I'm going to have to wait six years, aren't I?'

'Six years?'

'Until you qualify as a doctor.'

'What do you mean?'

'You know what I mean, Gordy,' she said, with an affectionate nudge in his ribs. 'Now, stop teasing me.'

'What's all this about six years?'

'Have you forgotten what you said to me in that tent?'

His mind reeled. His knees buckled. Gordy put a hand on the wall for support. His temples began to pound.

'Aah...yes. The tent. You and me. I remember now.'

'I should hope so,' she said with mock irritation. 'It was the most wonderful moment of my life. You asked me to marry you. I said I needed time to think it over. That's why I came after you, Gordy. I've made my decision and I'm here to give you my answer.'

Harriet kissed him full on the lips and wrapped her arms round his neck.

'Yes!' she breathed. 'I will!'

Suzie stood in front of the long mirror in the bathroom and appraised herself. She clicked her tongue in annoyance. She felt sure she was putting on weight. Suzie couldn't actually see any difference in her figure but she felt she was getting fat.

'Hurry up, Suzie!' shouted Bella. 'You'll be late!'

'Coming!'

'I'm going on ahead with Mark!'

'OK!' called Suzie.

She pulled a comb through her hair and took a last look at herself. When she got downstairs, Karlene was just leaving the house. They walked towards the hospital.

'Will you be seeing your friend again?' asked Suzie.

'Janie? Yes. Each and every day from now on.'

'That'll put a huge strain on you.'

'I don't mind,' said Karlene. 'She needs me. I only wish I could give her the right sort of help.'

'What do you mean?'

'I'm in the dark, Suzie. I've never been in a situation like this before. I'm frightened of saying or doing the wrong thing. I'd hate to upset Janie.'

'You won't do that. You're her lifeline.'

'That's what worries me most - Janie has such faith in me. Because I'm based at the hospital, she thinks I know everything. And I don't. I'm training to be a physio, that's all.'

'You've also got a natural gift for caring, Karlene.'

'It's not enough. I feel...out of my depth.'

'I can understand that.'

There was a long pause as Suzie thought about the problem. Karlene yawned. The late nights were taking their toll. Suzie snapped her fingers - suddenly thinking of a useful suggestion.

'Do the obvious thing, Karlene - take professional advice. You're in the right place.'

'I suppose I am.'

'Why not start with your tutor?' said Suzie. 'The one you like. Catherine something?'

'Catherine White.'

'She's been at the hospital for years. Chances are she's worked at the Burns Unit.'

'Catherine's worked everywhere.'

'There you are, then. Ask her opinion. I bet she could give you a lot of useful tips.'

'Yes,' said Karlene. 'Why didn't I think of that?'

'Because you've been completely tied up with Janie.'

'That's true. Thanks, Suzie. It's a great idea.' She thought it through. 'The Burns Unit calls on us all the time. Patients get very demoralised in there. Physios help to build up their strength and stamina. Make them feel better about themselves.'

'Isn't that what you have to do - make Janie feel better about herself?'

'Yeah, it is, Suzie. And it's an uphill task, I can tell you.'

They joined the main road and the hospital loomed ahead of them. Suzie always found the sight uplifting. She'd never regretted her decision to study there. Straightening her back, she inhaled deeply.

An ambulance went past them. 'Have they found out what started that fire?'

'No, not yet.'

'Mark said they suspected arson.'

'Yes,' said Karlene, gritting her teeth. 'In this case, I suppose they had to consider that.'

'Why?'

'Because Janie lives in a rough area. There are some vicious gangs roaming around. You know, neo-Nazis and people like that. Janie's house wouldn't be the first to be set alight out of sheer spite.'

'Who could do such a thing to them? Everyone says that the Palmer family are really nice people.'

'They're also black. Like me. In that area, the colour of your skin can sometimes make you a target. There are gangs of thugs operating there right now.'

'Do the police think it *was* a racist attack?'

Karlene sighed. 'That's always on the cards.'

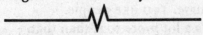

They were in the hospital canteen. When Mark brought the coffee over to her, Bella was reading his textbook again. He put the cups down and sat opposite her.

Pushing his spectacles up the bridge of his nose, he said, 'Right, ask me a difficult one.'

'They're *all* difficult, Mark,' she said, rolling her eyes. 'I can't answer any of them.'

'Try me.'

'You asked for it. "Eve Hudson, aged twenty-seven, is admitted to the Accident and Emergency Department, having slashed her wrists in a suicide attempt. Describe the nurse's role in the immediate care and treatment which Jan will receive." It's all yours, Mark.'

'First of all,' he said, confidently, 'I'd stop the bleeding with a firm dressing. Then I'd elevate the arms. Then I'd observe and record blood pressure, pulse rate, respiratory rate and skin colour for evidence of shock.'

Bella was astounded. 'That's absolutely right!'

'It also happens to be one of the cases I read about in bed last night.' He shrugged modestly. 'I got lucky. If you'd asked me anything to do with neurological problems or orthopaedic patients, I'd have been struggling.'

'I struggle with everything!' she moaned, putting the book aside. 'Am I really cut out to be a nurse, Mark?'

'Of course. You like people.'

'There's a lot more to it than that.'

'It'll come in time, Bella. You learn quickly.'

She added sugar to her coffee and stirred it.

'I'll never understand a case like that,' she said. 'Why on earth would anyone slash their wrists?'

'All sorts of reasons. Trouble at home. No money, nowhere to live. The feeling that you're sort of worthless...It does happen.'

'Nothing's worth killing yourself over.'

Mark smiled. 'I'll remind you of that if you have a disastrous love affair.'

'I'd never commit suicide over a guy!' she said with contempt. 'They grow on trees. Lose one, pick another.'

'That's a bit callous, isn't it?'

'It's practical. I lost Damian, I picked Neil.'

'What if it happened the other way round?'

'What do you mean?'

'Suppose a guy was madly in love with you... '

Bella grinned. 'The story of my life!'

'I'm serious,' he continued. 'Suppose you broke his heart and he took an overdose. Wouldn't you feel guilty?'

She thought it over. 'A bit, maybe.'

'Is that all?'

'It depends what'd happened between us.'

'Enough to make him kill himself.'

'No, Mark,' she said, firmly. 'It's not a fair question. No one can ever be responsible for someone else's suicide. In the end, it's their decision. Anyway, I always choose happy-go-lucky guys like Damian Holt. Suicidal types don't get near me.'

'How can you tell?'

'Instinct.'

'That doesn't always work.'

'Yes, it does,' she boasted. 'But I come back to my point, Mark. Life is such a wonderful thing. Why throw it away? Nobody's worth that!'

———————◁▷———————

The train left the station and slowly gathered speed. It was quite empty at that time of day. A tall, lean, curly-haired guy in jeans and a sweatshirt attracted no attention. He sat on his own, his forehead pressed against the window. Houses and factories shot past - but he saw none of them. His mind was fixed on something else.

He was still brooding when the inspector appeared.

'Tickets, please!' said the man. 'All tickets ready, please!'

The guy stood up as if in a trance. He put his ticket on his seat and walked towards the end of the compartment. The train was travelling fast now. He lowered a window to reach out for the handle and opened the door wide. A rush of air went through the compartment and alerted the inspector.

He lumbered down the aisle towards the young man.

'Shut that door!' he yelled. 'It's dangerous!'

The passenger waited until they passed an embankment.

'Stay there!' implored the man. 'Don't jump!'

But he was too late to stop him. At a point

60

where the embankment was steepest, the boy flung himself wildly from the train; he hit the other railway line, somersaulted a few times and rolled down the embankment like a lifeless doll.

It was over as quickly as that.

———————/\/\———————

'Oh, no! Not again!' said Suzie. 'Go away, Gordy!'

'Thanks for the welcome!' he said, sarcastically.

'The answer is N-O - No!'

'You don't even know what I'm going to ask, Suzie.'

'Yes, I do. I can tell from that hunted look on your face. You want me to ride shotgun again.'

'Well, not exactly.'

'You need me to protect you from your cast-off girlfriend, the one who works in Reception.' She shook her head. 'Sorry, Gordy. Get yourself out of this one.'

'All I wanted was a bit of advice.'

'Be honest with her. Tell her the truth.'

'It's not that easy.'

Gordy had tracked Suzie down in the garden at the rear of the hospital. She was feeding breadcrumbs to the birds. He'd hoped for a more sympathetic response from her.

'I've been looking for you everywhere, Suzie.'

'Then you were wasting your time.'

'Why aren't you having lunch in the canteen?'

'I didn't feel like any. I wanted some fresh air.'

She scattered the last of the crumbs on the lawn then scrunched up the paper bag she'd used for the stale bread. Dropping it into the nearest refuse bin, she glanced at him and sighed.

'All right, Gordy. Let's hear it.'

'I really need to talk to somebody,' he said. 'Bel would only laugh. And Karl is too mixed up with those people who got burned in the fire. I don't want to bother her.'

'What about Mark?'

'I couldn't discuss my love life with *him*.'

'Why not? He'd see it from the male point of view.'

'I want *your* point of view, Suzie.'

'Even if you don't agree with it?'

'Yes. I can rely on you to be objective.'

'I'll try,' she said. 'Let's walk, shall we?'

They strolled along the path that wound its way through the garden. Gordy searched for a way to express his dilemma.

'She jumped on me again this morning,' he said.

'Harriet?'

'I thought I'd given her the slip but she was waiting for me inside the medical school. It was grim. To cut a long story short, Harriet told me why she trailed me here. Apparently, I proposed to her.'

Suzie gulped. 'You *what*!'

'It sounds ridiculous, I know, but I do remember it vaguely.'

'When was this? Where?'

'Months ago,' he said. 'At a friend's party. His parents were out so we had the whole place to ourselves. I've never seen so much booze.'

'Say no more. You had too much.'

'There was this tent in the garden; couples kept sort of...drifting off there.'

'Spare me the sordid details.'

'I ended up in the tent with Harriet.'

'And asked her to marry you.'

'No...yes...maybe. I honestly can't remember.'

'Harriet obviously can.'

'I know!' he groaned. 'She thinks we're engaged.'

'Congratulations!'

'Don't make fun of me, Suzie. Tell me what to do.'

'Buy her a ring and keep your promise.'

'I can't do that!'

'Then explain why not,' said Suzie. 'As gently and tactfully as you can. You owe her that at the very least.'

He sighed, wearily. 'I suppose so.'

'And it's no good expecting sympathy from me,' she said, crisply. 'If you led her on, then you're in the wrong. You must have given her a reason to think it was a serious proposal. Why else would she go to all this trouble?'

'Harriet's in love with me.'

'Then let her down very lightly.'

'Somehow I can't find the right words.'

'Don't ask me to write the script.'

'Harriet's a nice enough girl,' said Gordy, 'but she will keep pestering me.'

'I don't want to rub it in,' she said, quietly, 'but you've done your share of pestering.'

'I know, I know, and I apologise, Suzie. I didn't mean to crowd you. Now I've been on the receiving end, I can see I must have been driving you crazy.'

'You were.' She smiled. 'Break it to her gently. Try to remember why you were together in the first place. I can't believe even you would propose to a girl on a first date.'

'We'd been going out for several weeks.'

'Then it wasn't a one-night-stand. You were an item.'

Gordy's face was a picture of misery. An ambulance siren cut through their conversation. Suzie looked towards Casualty.

'And don't feel so sorry for yourself,' she said. 'All you have to do is talk to a girl who has a crush on you. If you were in the back of that ambulance, you might *really* have something to worry about.'

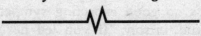

The doctor and his team were waiting as the stretcher was lifted out of the ambulance. The patient was deeply unconscious. His curly hair was clogged with blood, his head was bandaged. His clothing was torn and stained. The doctor could see at a glance he had sustained serious multiple injuries.

One of the paramedics followed them into Casualty.

'He jumped from a train travelling at forty miles an hour,' he explained. 'Miracle he's still in one piece.'

'It's a very long process,' she warned. 'It requires a lot of courage and endless patience.'

'Where does a physio come in?' said Karlene.

'We're only part of a team that includes clinical psychologists, occupational therapists, social workers and so on. The plastic surgeon is the general. We're the troops.'

Catherine White was a tall, slim, stately woman with dark hair peppered with grey. She'd been a physiotherapist for several years and had an enormous amount of experience. She also had a gift for passing on that experience to her students - without talking down to them.

Karlene liked her. The older woman was more than ready to advise her. She invited Karlene to her office.

'Get Janie to focus on her brother,' she said. 'He's the real victim here. Vance is the one who'll need most help.'

'I think Janie appreciates that.'

'His face will change completely. She has to accept that. We can only do so much at the hospital to rebuild the boy's confidence. Most of the work must be done at home by close family members and friends.'

'How can I help Janie in the short term?'

'Try to find out why she blames herself, Karlene. There has to be a reason. Keep probing gently.'

'I don't want to be too intrusive, Mrs White.'

'You have to be,' said the other. 'You can't treat any condition until you understand its causes. Janie is still in a state of shock. She's taken some horrendous blows in the last couple of days.'

'Being stuck with her aunt and uncle hasn't helped.'

'That's why she needs you as a prop and as an ally.' Mrs White stood up. 'My guess is, she's bottling something up. For her own sake, she has to let it out sooner or later. That's where you come in, Karlene.'

'I hope I'm up to it.'

'You will be, I'm sure.'

Karlene got up from her chair. 'Thanks, Mrs White.'

'If I can do anything else, just shout,' she offered, as they walked towards the door. 'Who's handling the case?'

'Mr Quentin.'

'I know him well. Donald Quentin is one of the finest plastic surgeons in the the business. Vance is lucky.' She gave a shrug. 'Not that he'll see it that way. The little boy will be overwhelmed by what's happening to him at first. Part of our job as physios is to raise his spirits. Give him back a sense of physical well-being. It's a base to build on.'

Karlene nodded. The long chat with Catherine White had been a revelation. It had also reminded Karlene why she'd chosen to be a physiotherapist in the first place.

'One more thing...'

'Yes, Mrs White.'

'Be ready for setbacks.'

'With Janie?'

'With the whole family,' she said, 'but mainly with Janie. She'll be volatile. Just when you think you're getting somewhere, she'll explode on you.'

'Back to square one.'

'Be prepared, that's all.'

'I will.'

'Hang in there, Karlene. She desperately needs a friend.'

———————⋀———————

It was curiosity that took Suzie into Reception. At least, that's what she told herself. After her chat with Gordy, she felt she had to see the girl who had struck such terror into him. So, at the end of her working day she made her way to Reception and studied the girls behind the desk.

Harriet was easy to pick out. She was the only receptionist under forty. Suzie was favourably impressed with her. She was attractive and neat with a wide, kind smile. Suzie felt a stab of envy when she saw how slim Harriet was. She was much prettier than some of the girls Gordy had taken out.

Suzie wandered close enough to hear her voice. Harriet was well-spoken. She was bright and friendly, handling all sorts of queries and phone calls. She stood up; an old man was asking for directions and Harriet had left her seat to show him the way.

Her slim figure aroused a pang of jealousy in Suzie. She turned away quickly and walked across Reception. She had just used Harriet as an excuse to go to the shop again.

Her eyes ran over the items in the window. She made her decision, waited until the shop was empty and went in.

'Yes, dear?' said the old lady behind the counter.

'I'd like some Jaffa Cakes, please.'

'Certainly. Here you are, dear.'

'Oh no,' said Suzie, 'not just one box - I'll take all you've got.'

Sister Killeen was feared but respected by the student nurses. She was a short, neat woman with a severe hairdo and a spotless uniform. She set high standards and could be very scathing if anyone fell below those standards. Bella had often felt the lash of the Killeen tongue. When she was singled out this time, Bella anticipated more trouble.

She was wrong. Sister Killeen complimented her.

'You did well on the Children's Ward,' she said.

'Thank you, Sister Killeen.'

'I had a good report. Very heartening.'

'I was only there for a short time,' said Bella. 'And they didn't let me do any real nursing. I was just a dogsbody.'

'There's no such thing in a hospital,' said Sister

Killeen with a flash of temper. 'However menial your tasks here, you are making an important contribution. We're all links in a chain.' She softened towards Bella. 'You came through with flying colours. That's why I've got another assignment for you.'

'Back to the Children's Ward?' said Bella, eagerly.

'I'm afraid not. The staffing problems are elsewhere. You and Mark Andrews will be helping out in Marlborough Ward.'

'Where's that, Sister Killeen?'

'In the East Wing. Third Floor.'

'What sort of work will we be doing?'

'I'll tell you that in a moment.'

Sister Killeen checked the watch pinned to her uniform.

'That's it, everybody. Thank you very much.'

The other students left their desks quickly and shuffled gratefully out. Bella and Mark stayed to hear more about their assignment. Staffing shortages were a common feature of hospital life. Students were often brought in to help out with basic tasks.

Sister Killeen waited until the others had gone.

'Report to Marlborough Ward first thing tomorrow.'

'Yes, Sister Killeen,' said Mark.

'You haven't told us what we'll be doing there, yet, Sister.'

'Conduct yourself in a professional manner, Bella.'

'Yes, Sister Killeen.'

'And do as you're told. Marlborough Ward is a small and very specialised ward. It's attached to the Psychiatric Unit.'

'Disturbed patients?' asked Mark.

'A couple of them are very disturbed,' said Sister Killeen.

'In what way?' said Bella.

'They attempted suicide.'

———————/\/———————

A three-hour operation had saved his life but left him desperately weak. The curly-haired patient was encased in plaster and covered in stitches. As well as a series of bone fractures, he'd suffered internal injuries. The surgeons had needed all their skills to bring him back from the brink of death. The patient was not in the most robust health and they noted signs of under-nourishment.

Gilbert Buchanan led the team in the operating theatre. One of the most distinguished figures at the hospital, he was brought in for really complicated cases. His expertise as a thoracic surgeon had been crucial on this occasion.

'That's it, everybody,' he said, standing back to admire his handiwork. 'We've done our bit. The rest is in the hands of the Almighty. Take Mr Devlin away.'

The patient was wheeled out by one of the porters.

'I'm glad that's over!' said Buchanan as he

pulled down his face mask. 'What a mess! He couldn't have had more injuries if he'd lain across the line and let the train run over him. We must feed the poor chap. By the look of that emaciated body, he almost starved himself to death as well.'

Another surgeon sounded more cynical.

'Was it worth all that trouble, I wonder?'

'Of course, it was,' said the senior man.

'He tried to commit suicide, Gilbert. By jumping from a moving train. We can't keep someone alive if he's that determined to die.'

'Mr Devlin may have second thoughts now.'

'Suppose he doesn't? Suppose he tries again?'

Gilbert Buchanan stroked his goatee beard and smiled.

'We'll be ready for him,' he said, blithely. 'If it's at all possible, we'll patch him up. It's not our job to make moral judgements about people. Patients are patients. Our task is to save each and every one of them.'

———————⋀\/———————

The Caribbean Club was a long, low, ramshackle building with a corrugated iron roof. Graffiti covered the outside walls and one of the windows was boarded up. The place looked rundown.

Inside, however, it was a very different story. The rooms were warm and well-decorated. Everything was meticulously clean. Karlene felt the welcoming atmosphere as soon as she let herself in through the front door.

'Hello, stranger!' said a cheery voice.

'Hello, Madge.'

'Haven't seen you around for a few weeks.'

'No,' said Karlene. 'I've been very busy lately.'

'Don't desert us, will you?'

Madge was a big, jolly woman in her sixties. She wore a smart red dress and a pair of fur-lined slippers. Even at the regular dances at the club, she kept her slippers on. Madge was pottering noisily about in the coffee bar when Karlene walked in.

'You too early,' said Madge. 'We're not open.'

'That's OK. I only came to see you.'

Madge chuckled. 'That's nice!'

'How are your bad feet?'

'They still on the end of my legs,' said the old woman with a throaty laugh. 'But they do hurt sometimes.'

'Sit down more often.'

'Don't get no chance. I work here every evening.'

'That's what I came to talk to you about,' said Karlene. 'You must've heard about the fire in Cameron Street.'

'Oh, yes!' said Madge. 'It was terrible! House gutted. Greg Palmer killed. His wife and son badly burned. It was a tragedy. I'm starting a collection for them.'

'It's Janie that worries me at the moment.'

'That girl was *so* lucky not to be there.'

'What time did she leave the club on the night of the fire. Did you see her go?'

'How could I, Karlene?'

'Weren't you on duty?'

'I'm *always* on duty,' said Madge, proudly. 'This place'd fall down if I wasn't here to hold it up. Janie didn't leave the club that night 'cos she never came in the first place.'

'Are you sure, Madge?'

The old woman nodded. 'My feet may be falling off but my eyes are still sharp. I see everybody who comes through that door. Janie wasn't here. She'd never dare to come to the club without speaking to me.'

'No, of course not.'

Karlene was puzzled. Where had Janie been that night?

'What's the news from the hospital?' asked Madge.

'Mrs Palmer is recovering slowly but Vance is in a bad state. We won't be seeing him around for a long time.'

'I sent Get Well cards to both of them,' said Madge. 'Everyone at the club signed them. We were so sorry.'

Karlene looked up into her kind face. Madge was a mother figure for the whole black community. She would organise a lot of support for the Palmer family. It would be very reassuring.

'Thanks, Madge. Have to be on my way now.'

'Come again, soon.'

'I will.'

Karlene left. The chat with Madge had been both

enlightening and disturbing. Karlene wondered why Janie had lied to her. What was the girl hiding?

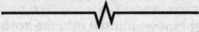

The walk back to the house took her past the end of Cameron Street. Everything was quiet now. No fire engine, no ambulances, no police cars, no crowd - and of course, no fire. Karlene was about to walk on down the main road when she saw a lone figure in the distance, standing outside the burnt-out house.

It was Janie. She was staring blankly at her home.

Karlene turned into the street and walked towards her. Janie stood motionless. The house looked desolate in the evening light. Its front door and ground floor windows had been boarded up but the upper windows were blackened holes. The roof had been burned to a cinder. Everything inside the building had been completely destroyed.

Janie stood there in silence. Tears poured down her face. Guilt consumed her. It was almost as if she was deliberately forcing herself to look in order to be punished.

Karlene put an arm round her shoulder.

'Come on, Janie,' she said. 'You've seen enough.'

Gordy Robbins let himself into the house and shut the door behind him with a sense of relief. He could relax at last. After his encounter with Harriet, he'd been on edge all day. She had completely rattled him.

At first, he'd regretted his decision to confide in Suzie. He hoped that she would be on his side but she was much too fair-minded for that. On reflection, Gordy saw that her advice was sound. He had to confront Harriet and be frank with her. It was time to disentangle himself gently from his engagement.

'Engagement!' he groaned. 'I don't want to marry *anyone*.'

At least he could count on Suzie's discretion. She wouldn't gossip to the others. If Bella got to hear about his moment of madness in the tent, she would tease him unmercifully. Gordy still hadn't forgiven her for the fake telephone call. He wanted revenge.

An idea came to him and he laughed out loud.

'Yes! Yes!' he said. 'That'll teach her!'

He ran upstairs to prepare the 'surprise'.

—⋀—

'Come in with me, Karlene!' begged Janie. 'Please.'

'But she'll want to see you on your own.'

'I'm scared.'

'Of your own mum?'

'I'm afraid she'll blame me.'

'That's ridiculous,' said Karlene, gently. 'Your mum is desperate to see you, Janie. She'll be so pleased that one member of her family escaped the flames. Think how much worse it'd be if you were lying there in the Burns Unit as well.'

Janie twisted her scarf between her fingers.

'Sometimes, I wish that I was!'

When Karlene found her in Cameron Street, she had brought her friend back to the hospital. It was not the moment to challenge her about her whereabouts on the night of the fire. Janie was clearly in a very delicate state. She was being allowed to visit her mother properly for the first time. She had seen Mrs Palmer through an observation window and they had waved to each other, but that was all.

Her mother was well enough now to receive visitors.

'What do I say, Karlene?' asked Janie.

'Tell her how you feel. Tell her you love her.'

Janie was anxious. 'But does she still love *me*?'

'Of course she does!'

'But I let them all down.'

'Stop saying that, Janie. It's not true. Just think of them. Your mum will need to lean heavily on you from now on. So will Vance. You've got to be *strong* for them. You've got to show them they can count on you.'

Janie nodded. 'You're right, Karlene.'

The door of the waiting room opened and Linda Naylor came in, dabbing at her eyes with a handkerchief. Her face hardened when she saw Janie.

'Where've *you* been?' she accused.

'For a walk.'

'Your mum's been asking for you. You should have been here. Why can't you ever do the right thing, Janie?'

'I'm going in there right now,' said Janie, sulkily. 'On my own. I didn't want to see her with you.' She glanced towards the door. 'How is she?'

'Very poorly. I had a shock when I first saw her.'

'Could she talk to you?'

'Oh, yes. That's about all she *was* able to do. Your mother's in a bad way. Don't do anything to upset her. Behave for once.'

Karlene saw the worried look on Janie's face. 'Excuse us, Mrs Naylor,' she said.

She turned to leave the room with her friend. Janie's aunt was only upsetting her. Janie needed to be calm for this visit. On their way to the Burns Unit, Karlene did her best to reassure her friend. When they reached the door of the ward, Karlene stopped.

'In you go, Janie,' she said. 'I'll wait here.'

'Promise?'

'Of course. Give her my best wishes, won't you?'

'Sure.'

Karlene gave Janie a squeeze of encouragement then pushed her gently in through the door. A nurse came to meet her and led her to the side ward to see her mother. Janie was very nervous and was licking her lips which felt suddenly dry. She had no idea what to expect.

She braced herself as she stepped into the ward. She was shocked at what she saw. Her mother was swathed in bandages and connected to a drip. Her face was badly swollen, her eyes half-shut. She seemed very weak.

'Janie...' she croaked.

It was obviously painful for her to speak but there was relief and love in her voice. Very gingerly, she lifted an arm and held out a bandaged hand. Janie walked to her bedside and let her mother's hand rest lightly between her own palms.

'Hello, Mum,' she said. 'How are you?'

'Not too bad.'

'I've been worrying myself sick.'

'So have I, Janie,' said her mother, as a tear trickled down her face. 'I've missed you so much. It's just so good to see you again!'

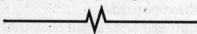

When Bella and Mark got back from the hospital, Gordy was preparing the evening meal. He gave them a cheerful welcome.

'I hope you're both hungry,' he said.

'Famished,' said Bella. 'What is it?'

'Home-made pizza.'

'Sounds good,' said Mark, sniffing. 'Smells good, too.'

'There'll be plenty for everybody,' said Gordy.

Bella grinned. 'In that case, maybe we should ask Harriet to join us. I'm dying to meet this girl.'

'Don't start all that again,' said Gordy, wearily.

'I'm serious. She must be really weird.'

'Bella!' he warned.

'Any girl who fancies you is peculiar,' she taunted.

'I thought she was very nice,' said Mark.

'Nice but nutty. I mean, Harriet came to the hospital just to be near the man of her dreams. Gordy! Instead of working in Reception, she ought to be referred for psychiatric reports.'

'Don't be mean, Bella,' said Mark.

'No,' added Gordy. 'Or I'll put arsenic in your pizza and ground glass in your coffee.'

'Forget about Harriet,' advised Mark. 'Gordy has.'

Bella giggled. 'But she hasn't forgotten about him, has she? There's Gordy, playing the field at the medical school. And all this time, he has a skeleton in the cupboard.'

Gordy spluttered and turned back to the stove.

'Where's Suzie?' asked Mark.

'Up in her room,' said Gordy. 'Said she wouldn't be eating with us this evening. Feels a bit off colour.'

'What's wrong with her?' wondered Bella.

'Don't know. She looks great to me.'

'That's what you used to say about Harriet!'

'Bella!'

He turned to threaten her with a wooden spoon but she'd already vanished from the kitchen. Still laughing, she ran upstairs, calling, 'I'll just get changed! Won't be long!'

Gordy smiled to himself and opened the oven door.

Bella let herself into her room. She tossed her bag on to the bed then slipped off her coat. After wearing a uniform all day, she was anxious to get into something more comfortable. Kicking off her shoes she crossed to her cupboard.

She opened the door, thinking what she might wear.

'Arghhhhhh!'

Her scream was ear-splitting. It brought Suzie and Mark racing into her room. Bella was petrified. Hanging in her cupboard was a full-size human skeleton. A lighted torch had been fixed in the skull so that the eyes glowed eerily.

Suzie put an arm round Bella. Mark switched off the torch.

'It's only Matilda,' he said. 'Gordy's skeleton.'

Bella shivered. 'It gave me the fright of my life!'

'I'm not surprised,' said Suzie.

'I opened the door and - there it was!'

Gordy strode nonchalantly into her room.

'Oh, dear!' he said with a mocking grin. 'Bella's got a skeleton in her cupboard as well.'

'You...you...' she shrieked and grabbing a pillow, chased him down the stairs.

When the anaesthetic had worn off, he regained consciousness for a few minutes. Rob Devlin had no idea where he was or how he got there. His mind was very fuzzy at first. All he could remember was getting on to the train.

He tried to move but his whole body seemed to be encased in plaster. His head was heavily bandaged. Even the tiniest shift of position produced a dull pain.

His eyelids felt like lead but he made an effort to open them. Bright light made him screw up his eyes in pain but as he got used to the glare, he saw he was looking up into the smiling face of a man with a goatee beard.

'Hello, old chap,' said Gilbert Buchanan. 'Just dropped in to see how you're getting on.'

The young man tried to speak. His words were slurred but the surgeon knew exactly what he was asking.

'You're in hospital, Mr Devlin,' he explained. 'You're going to need plenty of rest. Post-operative recuperation, we call it. We had to put you back together again. Like a jigsaw.'

Rob Devlin dozed off for a minute then surfaced once more. The surgeon was still examining him.

'Don't worry,' said Gilbert Buchanan. 'We'll take good care of you. After all the trouble you've given us, we're not going to let you slip through our fingers now. How do you feel?'

The patient's lips moved but his words were jumbled.

'Try to get some more sleep, Mr Devlin.'

Rob's lips trembled again as he made a huge effort to speak.

'Don't tax your strength. Lie back and relax.'

Rob Devlin remembered something else now. The jump from the train and the collision with the railway line. The leap of death. His mind was on fire. 'I'm still alive!' he thought. 'They've cheated me. They've brought me back. I don't want to be here! I can't stand it any more. What's the point?' He used the last ounce of energy to squeeze out a desperate request.

'Please...let me...*die*.'

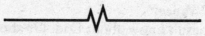

Karlene was waiting for her when she finally came out. Janie seemed much calmer. An hour with her mother had been distressing in some ways but reassuring in others.

'Can we go somewhere?' asked Janie.

'Of course, why?'

'Aunty Linda's in the waiting room. I'm not ready to face her yet. I need time, Karlene.'

'Follow me.'

Karlene led her along a corridor until they found an alcove with some plastic chairs in it. They sat down.

'How was your mum?'

'She looked awful.'

'Mr Quentin explained that,' said Karlene, quickly. 'He said that her burns looked far worse than they really were. They'll heal naturally in time.'

'I hope so.'

'If your mum wasn't getting better, they wouldn't be thinking about letting her go home.'

'That's true.'

Janie was subdued but less haunted than before.

'What did you talk about?' asked Karlene.

'Dad, mostly.'

'How's your mum taking it?'

'She still can't believe it.'

'Your Dad was a very brave man, Janie.'

'He knew how much Vance loved that puppy.' She lowered her voice. 'They haven't told him yet.'

'Who? Vance?'

'He doesn't know about Dad. Or about Coco.'

'It'll be a horrible shock.'

'That's why they've kept it from him,' said Janie. 'He's just not strong enough to cope with it all. Vance is sedated a lot of the time. To take away the pain.'

'He'll have to face up to it one day, Janie.'

'I know. We all will, Karlene.'

She looked dazed as she stared out of the window. For a few minutes Karlene said nothing. When she turned back to her friend again, Janie's expression was questioning.

'What were you doing there?' she asked.

'Doing where?'

'In Cameron Street. When you found me.'

'I was on my way home. From the club.'

Janie started guiltily. 'You've been to the club?'

'I called in to have a chat with Madge,' said Karlene. 'She's still having trouble with those bunions of hers. By the way, she got everyone to sign Get Well cards for your mum and Vance. They're all thinking about you at the club.'

Janie looked at Karlene, almost inviting the question.

'You didn't go there that night, did you?' said Karlene.

'No,' said Janie.

'Will you tell me where you *did* go?'

'I can't...I can't, Karlene.'

Karlene felt her friend was ready to confide in her at last. Seeing her mother had changed Janie's manner. She was less defensive and much more open. Once she was back with her aunt again, she would retreat into her shell. Karlene decided she had to take the opportunity while it was there.

'Tell me about it, Janie, please,' she said. 'Where were you that night? What was so important that it kept you out so late?'

Janie's look changed to one of hostility and she got to her feet. She felt betrayed. She was breathing fast and trembling. Karlene got up and tried to calm her by putting a hand on her shoulder.

'Don't touch me!' yelled Janie. 'I hate you!'

She turned and ran off down the corridor.

CHAPTER NINE

'You wait!' said Bella. 'I'll get my own back somehow.'

'Why not just forget the whole thing?' said Mark.

'No way! Gordy put that skeleton in my cupboard!'

'Only because you played a wicked trick on him. Pretending to be on the phone to that old flame of his.'

'That was just harmless fun.'

'He nearly freaked out.'

'How do you think *I* felt when I saw that skeleton glaring at me with yellow eyes? I almost fainted.'

A good night's sleep had not quietened Bella down. She was still seething about what Gordy had done. As she and Mark walked in through the main gate of the hospital that morning, she was smouldering.

'I'll give Harriet Collins our phone number.'

'That'd be mean, Bella.'

'I know!' she said in triumph. 'I'll sneak Harriet into the house and hide her in his wardrobe. When Gordy opens it at night, he'll find her grinning at him.' She was grinning herself now.

As they went into the main block, she grabbed his arm.

'Point her out, Mark.'

'No, Bella.'

'She's one of the receptionists, isn't she? I want to see her.'

'It might be better if you didn't.'

But Bella had already spotted Harriet. She was the only blond. Bella stared at her open-mouthed.

'She's really attractive,' she said.

'That's what I thought.'

'Gordy usually goes for ugly girls with long hair and bad skin. Harriet's not like that at all.'

'Come on,' said Mark. 'Or we'll be late.'

He pulled her towards the lift and eased her inside. It was their first morning on Marlborough Ward and he wanted to be punctual. Sister Killeen would monitor their performance very carefully. Mark didn't want to give her any excuse for unleashing one of her famous tempers.

When they reached the third floor, they walked to the East Wing. Bella perked up at once. Like Mark, she was looking forward to getting some more practical experience.

'Good morning!'

Sister McCrandle was waiting for them outside the ward. She was a Scotswoman in her thirties with a gap between her front teeth. Her manner was a bit overpowering but she seemed friendly enough.

'Good morning!' they said in unison.

'Sister Killeen sent us,' added Mark.

'So I understand.' She sized them up. 'You must be Mark Andrews and this is Della Benton.'

'Bella Denton,' corrected the other.

'I beg your pardon, dear. I'm Sister McCrandle.'

'We're very glad to be here,' said Mark. 'Sister Killeen didn't say too much about what we have to do.'

'Anything and everything.'

'That suits us,' he volunteered.

'Good. Let me show you the lay-out.'

Marlborough Ward was a small, square room with a few sidewards and offices leading off it. A couple of the beds were empty. Bella and Mark looked at the patients. All of them were male, most were quite young.

'Right,' said Sister McCrandle. 'There it is. You can start by changing the two beds at the far end of the ward. You'll find fresh linen in the laundry room.' They nodded. 'Don't talk to the patients,' she insisted. 'That's not part of your job. Just be friendly. You have no training as psychiatric nurses and some of them need extremely careful handling. Do you understand?'

'Yes, Sister McCrandle,' said Mark.

'What's in the sidewards?' asked Bella.

'Our Critical Care Unit. We only have one patient there at the moment. A boy - a suicide attempt.'

Bella's eyes widened. 'What did he do?'

'He jumped out of a moving train.'

Bella tried to peer through the observation window but Sister McCrandle tapped her hard on the shoulder. Her tone became very menacing.

'Don't stare, nurse,' she ordered. 'This is not a

zoo. I've given you a job. Get on with it.'

━━━━━━⋁━━━━━━

'I felt such a fool,' admitted Karlene. 'I blew it.'

'No, you didn't,' said Suzie.

'I rushed things.'

'Janie will come back to you.'

'I doubt it. I frightened her off good and proper.'

'You're her friend. You're trying to help her.'

'That's not what Janie thinks.'

They had met by accident in the lunch hour. Karlene was coming down the stairs as Suzie was going up them. They began to chat and Karlene confided her worries.

'Mrs White did warn me,' she remembered. 'Sudden shifts in mood. Just when I hoped I was getting somewhere with Janie, she flips and runs off.'

'Your question was obviously too near the mark. So what's the next stage, Karlene?'

'I honestly don't know,' she said. 'My first impulse was to go after Janie and reason with her but that would've done no good. So I'm giving her time to calm down.'

'Very wise.'

'I'm not so sure. I'm really floundering, Suzie.'

'Janie *needs* you.'

'Does she? I only seem to be making matters worse.'

'No,' said Suzie. 'Deep down, she needs you badly. And Janie will soon realise it. Don't chase her, Karlene. Wait until she comes back to you.'

'*If* she comes back.'

'She will. In the meantime, take a breather.'

'I could certainly do with it, Suzie.'

'You've been late three nights running.'

'Yeah. Missed all the fun, by the sound of it.'

'Fun?'

'Bella says that Matilda turned up in her cupboard.'

'That wasn't fun,' said Suzie. 'It was frightening. Gordy's always using that skeleton to scare someone. Last night it was Bella's turn.'

'If I know her, she'll soon get her own back.'

'I wish they'd stop. It's getting on my nerves.'

'And mine.'

'We must make peace between them.'

'Knock their heads together, you mean?'

'That's what they both deserve,' said Suzie with a smile. 'No, the problem only flared up when this girl appeared on the scene.'

'Gordy's ex?'

'Harriet Collins. Once she goes out of his life, Bella won't be able to tease him about her.'

'But *will* she get out of his life?'

Suzie nodded confidently. 'I think so. My guess is that Gordy will be sorting it all out very soon.'

'I've only got an hour,' she said. 'We'll have to be quick.'

'This won't take long, Harriet.'

'I was really pleased to get your note.'

'Er...were you?'

'It was so romantic, Gordy.'

'All I did was to scribble a few lines.'

'They're engraved on my heart - "Meet me at one o'clock. Jacaranda Cafe." I was knocked out.' She looked around. 'It's a lovely place. Nice and quiet.'

'That's why I chose it.'

Gordy decided to stop running away from her. As long as he did that, Harriet would keep on his trail like a bloodhound. His only escape lay in telling her the truth. It might hurt at first but he persuaded himself that she'd be better off in the long run. So would he!

A cheerful young waitress came up to their table.

'Ready to order yet?'

'No, not yet,' said Gordy.

'I am,' said Harriet. 'Ham and mushroom omelette.'

'Make that two,' added Gordy, dismissively.

'With a side salad?' said the waitress.

Harriet nodded. Gordy shook his head. The girl took away the menus. Harriet reached out to touch his hand.

'This is my fantasy come true, Gordy.'

'That's what I wanted to talk about.'

'Your note said it all.'

She lowered her eyelids and blew him a kiss. He grabbed his glass of beer and took a restorative gulp. Gordy groped around in his memory for the speech he'd rehearsed.

'This can't go on, Harriet,' he said.

'It can if we want it to, darling.'

'You don't seem to understand my position.'

'Sure I do,' she said. 'That's why I don't expect to spend every minute of the day with you. I know your work comes first and I respect that.'

'I can't be tied down.'

'I'd never do that, Gordy,' she promised. 'You can come and go as you please. All I want is to spend some time with you now and then. Just like we're doing at this moment. I don't want to live with you or anything.'

'That's a relief!'

'Until the great day comes, that is.'

'Great day?'

'In six years' time. Wedding bells.'

'Harriet...'

'I've chosen the hymns already. And the dress.'

'Let's not rush things.'

'Six years is not rushing things,' she purred. 'It'll give us time to get to know each other even better. We'll sort of...grow together.'

He had a long sip of beer to give him courage.

'It's just not on, Harriet,' he blurted out.

'What isn't?'

'Everything. You - me - wedding bells in six years.'

'We'll get married sooner, if you want to.'

'No!'

'Doctor and Mrs Gordon Robbins. It has a ring to it.'

A death knell! he thought to himself.

'We'll be so happy,' she gushed. 'We'll do all the things we talked about.'

'Talked about?'

'In that tent.'

'I don't remember much talking in there, Harriet.'

She squeezed his hand. 'You said enough.'

Gordy was starting to lose his nerve. He took a third drink of beer and tried to sound decisive.

'We've got to stop seeing each other, Harriet.'

'Why?'

'Because I've got too many doubts about us.'

'That's why I want a long engagement,' she said. 'So that we can iron out all the difficulties beforehand.'

'We are *not* getting engaged!'

He banged the table for effect and knocked the salt cellar on to the floor. As he bent to pick it up, he caught his head on the edge of the table. He rubbed his scalp.

'There, there!' she cooed. 'Let me kiss it better.'

'Did you hear what I said, Harriet?'

'Yes. We're not getting engaged just yet.'

'Not now. Not ever.'

'You'll come round to the idea in time, Gordy. I did.'

'Harriet,' he whispered. 'I don't want to marry you.'

'That's not what you said in that tent.'

'Why can't we just be friends?'

'Because we've gone beyond that stage,' she argued. 'I know that you don't love me as much as I love you. But you will, eventually. I'll *make* you. I'm going to be the perfect wife for you. It's my mission in life.'

'Oh...no!'

Gordy put his hands over his eyes in despair. He'd lost the initiative once again. Harriet burbled on. Instead of getting rid of her, he'd managed to get even more involved.

Squirming in frustration, he made a solemn vow to himself never to go in a rotten tent with a girl again!

Mark and Bella were kept very busy in Marlborough Ward. They fetched, carried, washed, cleaned and did all kinds of mundane chores. Mark moved around with quiet efficiency but Bella's curiosity got the better of her.

'That patient in the end bed took an overdose,' she whispered.

'How do you know?'

'I read his chart.'

'Bella!'

'We're here to learn, aren't we?'

'Sister McCrandle told us not to talk to patients.'

'I just happened to see their charts, didn't I?' she said, artlessly. 'He's the other suicide Sister McCrandle mentioned.'

They were in the storeroom at the end of the

ward. Sister McCrandle had given them a list of supplies to put on a trolley in readiness for the doctor's ward round.

'The one that fascinates me is Rob Devlin. That young guy in the Critical Care Unit.'

'Keep away from there, Bella!'

'What makes someone jump from a train like that?'

'Forget him.'

'I don't believe anyone's life can be *that* bad.'

'Yours will be if Sister McCrandle catches you spying on the patients.'

'But she won't catch me, will she?' said Bella with a grin. 'I'm too clever by half.'

She put her head out of the door and saw the sister had disappeared. She strolled casually along to the observation window of the Critical Care Unit and peered in.

Rob Devlin was lying on his back. Tubes and wires connected him to a machine. A nurse was in the room with him but her back was turned as she made notes on a chart. Bella looked at the still figure and sighed in sympathy.

She was about to move away when she noticed that he was awake. He opened his eyes and saw that the nurse was distracted. Reaching out a hand, he grabbed the wires and tubes and gave them a sharp tug.

Bella was horrified. He had just disconnected himself from the life support machine. Rob Devlin desperately wanted to die.

CHAPTER TEN

Bella was mesmerised. For a few moments she couldn't move. She stared through the glass. There was no mistake. The patient had disconnected all his life-supporting tubes and wires. Rob Devlin was choosing a less violent way to die this time. Bella tried to pull herself together. A nurse's job was to preserve life, not to watch it ebb away.

Her first instinct was to scream but that would only alarm the patients in the main ward. Instead, Bella knocked on the observation window to attract the nurse's attention.

She looked up and saw Bella gesturing wildly.

'There!' she mouthed. 'Look at him!' She pointed at Rob.

The nurse turned round to the patient and saw what had happened. She responded quickly. Gathering up the tubes and wires, she reconnected them to the life support machine, checking all the dials to make sure that everything was functioning satisfactorily again.

'Thank goodness!' said Bella. 'We mustn't let him die.'

Rob Devlin made a feeble grab for the machine but the nurse was too quick for him. Catching his arm, she tucked it gently by his side then brought a strap over the bed to secure both his arms. He was unable to move either of his hands now.

Bella watched everything with admiration. The

nurse had been so cool under pressure. Now she picked up the telephone and made a call. Thirty seconds later, a doctor hurried into the unit with Sister McCrandle at his heels. He examined Rob and double-checked that the machine was working properly. He nodded his approval.

The nurse explained what had happened and pointed to Bella. Sister McCrandle stared at her. Bella had seen that look in Sister Killeen's eye. She wondered if it was part of the standard issue for hospital sisters along with their uniforms.

Bella was soon hauled off to Sister McCrandle's office.

'Well, my girl,' she said, 'I don't know whether to tell you off or congratulate you.'

'I just happened to be passing the observation window.'

'Lucky for the patient that you were.'

'It was a shock,' said Bella. 'I couldn't believe what I was seeing. Right in front of my eyes.'

'You get used to that sort of thing here. If they're really determined, they'll try again as soon as they can. That's why we always keep the windows locked. To stop any of the patients jumping out.'

'I just feel so sorry for him, Sister McCrandle.'

'Yes, Bella. It's a sad case. They always are.'

'Who is Mr Devlin?'

'We don't know much about him,' said the sister. 'He was on a train and he jumped out as it was travelling at speed past a high embankment.

That's all they told us.'

'Doesn't he have a family and friends?'

'The police are still trying to track them down.'

'He must have *someone* who cares for him.'

'That's *our* job, too.'

'He's only about my age, Sister McCrandle. That's what I can't get over. Why isn't he like me, with so much to look forward to in life?'

'If we knew the answer to that, we wouldn't have quite so many cases like Mr Devlin's in here.'

'I just can't imagine feeling that desperate.'

'Nor me,' admitted the sister, sadly. 'It's a question of temperament and circumstances, I suppose. Perhaps we are simply born with a more positive outlook.'

'Is there any chance I could speak to him?'

'No, Bella. We couldn't permit that, I'm afraid. As you saw, he's in a very disturbed condition.' She became brisk. 'Blenheim Ward is short of beds. We can spare two. Take them from the far end.'

'Yes, Sister McCrandle.'

'Ask Mark to give you a hand.'

'I will, don't worry.'

Bella started to leave but the sister's voice detained her.

'As for Mr Devlin, you did the right thing. Thank you.'

'Will you tell Sister Killeen that, please?'

Sister McCrandle smiled. 'Yes. I'll tell her.'

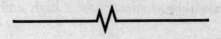

98

When Karlene crossed the car park that morning, she was tempted to drop into the main block of the hospital to see if Janie was there. Karlene's conscience had given her a troubled night. She was still angry with herself for scaring Janie away. The girl was desperate for help and Karlene was the one person who could give it to her. But everything depended on trust and Janie no longer trusted her.

Don't chase her, Karlene. Wait until she comes to you.

Suzie's advice echoed in her ears. Karlene would not go searching for Janie. She walked away from the main block.

'Karlene!' called a voice. 'Wait a minute!'

She turned to see Janie's aunt hurrying across to her.

'Good morning, Mrs Naylor.'

'I was hoping to bump into you.'

'Isn't Janie with you today?'

'No,' said the other woman, brusquely. 'I left her at home in disgrace. Janie's been very disobedient.'

'Disobedient?'

'We sent her to bed early last night and she sneaked out of the house. Didn't get back until midnight.'

'Where'd she been, Mrs Naylor?'

'She wouldn't say. Denzil - that's my husband - was furious.'

'He would be.'

'We were so worried about Janie,' she said. 'I mean, you know the kind of area it is. A young girl out on her own at night. Anything could have happened to her.'

'Didn't Janie have any explanation?'

'She went for a walk, she said. Because she felt trapped in the house. *Trapped*! We've taken that girl in and given her all she needs. Do we get a word of thanks from her? No!'

'I'm sure she's grateful, Mrs Naylor. But she's also very confused and upset at the moment.'

'So am I, Karlene. I've got so much to cope with.'

'Of course.'

'Janie was funny all day yesterday,' continued Mrs Naylor. 'And she was in a right old temper when we left the hospital in the evening. Did you notice anything?'

Karlene was not going to confide in this woman. Janie's aunt saw everything from her own point of view. Her dislike of her niece was starting to come through strongly. She disapproved of everything that Janie did or said.

'No,' said Karlene. 'Janie seemed nervous, that's all.'

'I'll be glad when that girl goes back to school. We don't want her slopping around the house all day.' She glanced at the main block. 'And when they let her mother out, we're going to have an even bigger problem. *All* our lives have been changed by that fire.'

Karlene nodded. 'Do they know what caused it yet?'

'Yes,' she said. 'It was something electrical, they think. I don't understand these things. To do with faulty wiring.'

'So the fire wasn't deliberate?'

'No - thank heavens!'

'That's good news.'

'It's a big load off our minds, Karlene. The police had to consider that it might have been arson. I mean, you know some of the people who hang around that area. They'd stop at nothing if they had a grudge against you. We were so relieved.' She shrugged. 'But it doesn't alter the fact that the house was burned to the ground.'

'The insurance will cover that, surely?'

'It won't help my sister-in-law.'

'It's bound to. They'll give Mrs Palmer the money to have the house rebuilt. They might even pay for her to stay somewhere else while the work is going on.'

'No chance of that.'

'Why not?'

'Because they didn't own the house,' said Linda Naylor. 'They were only tenants. It's the landlord who gets all the insurance money and he's a miserable old skinflint. He won't give them a penny.'

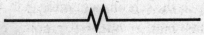

Vance Palmer had the same nightmare again. It was just as intense and vivid.

He went rushing into the house to rescue Coco and was confronted by a wall of flame. He was on fire.

With a silent scream, he woke up. He'd been given a pain-killing drug while the doctor removed the dressing on his face. It had made him drowsy. The boy's arms and legs were strapped down gently so that he wouldn't damage the burned areas of his body with any scratching or sudden movement.

The surgeon's voice was soft and reassuring.

'Almost there, Vance,' he said. 'One last pad.'

Vance only half-heard him. The figure who was bending over his bed in a white coat was a blur.

'That's it, Vance. Good boy! You're a model patient.'

Donald Quentin was a short, stout man with a round face but his podgy hands moved with deft precision. When the dressing was removed, the surgeon inspected Vance's facial injuries with the utmost care. A nurse stood beside him.

'This case is quite a challenge for me,' said the surgeon.

'Yes, Mr Quentin.'

'It'll be rewarding work. Rebuilding a face always is. But it'll be a long haul.'

'At least he's out of danger now.'

'Oh, yes. Vance is a strong, healthy boy. His mother tells me that he's an excellent swimmer. Won a cup at the school swimming gala. Good all-round sportsman, Vance, aren't you?'

Vance heard his name this time but could make no reply.

'That makes a big difference to my work. The success of skin grafts depends on a good blood supply in the recipient area. We shouldn't have any problems there.'

'No, Mr Quentin.'

The surgeon finished his scrutiny and sighed.

'Thank heavens we can do all this on the National Health,' he murmured. 'The NHS has its critics, I know, but I'm always grateful for it at moments like this. Vance deserves the best possible help,' said Mr Quentin. 'If he had to pay for all the complicated surgery involved, it would cost an absolute fortune!'

Vance was not listening. He was fast asleep again, dreaming of happier times with Coco and with his family.

―――――⋀―――――

It was the end of a long and interesting day in Marlborough Ward. Mark was wheeling a trolley into the corridor when the lift opened. A tall, elegant man stepped out. Mark recognised him at once and stared at him with curiosity.

Gilbert Buchanan had legendary status in the hospital. Mark had heard all the stories about the surgeon. He felt he was looking at a minor god.

'Good afternoon, young man.'

'Good afternoon, sir.'

'Sister McCrandle about?'

'I think she's in her office.'

'Thank you.'

Gilbert Buchanan smiled at him and walked past. As soon as the surgeon went into the office, Mark went back to the ward and beckoned to Bella.

'Do you know who's in there with Sister McCrandle?'

'Who?'

'Gilbert Buchanan.'

'I think he operated on Mr Devlin.'

'He *spoke* to me, Bella. I mean, I actually met him.'

'He's only a surgeon,' she chided. 'I know they do an amazing job but it's not like meeting real stars. *Take That*, for instance, or Maria Carey.'

'Bella!'

'I've always wanted to meet Lisa Stansfield.'

'Gilbert Buchanan is a genius,' said Mark. 'I must see him in action for a minute.'

They walked up to the Critical Care Unit and pretended to be sorting out the items on a trolley. Both of them kept an eye on the observation window. The nurse was standing beside the bed when Sister McCrandle brought the surgeon in.

Gilbert Buchanan bent over the patient and examined him carefully. Rob Devlin appeared to be asleep. The surgeon checked all the dressings on his wounds and looked at the dials on the life-support machine. He took a chart from the nurse and glanced down it.

Handing the chart back, he gave a series of instructions to the nurse. Nodding obediently, she wrote down all the details. Mark and Bella were so fascinated that they gave up any pretence of doing anything else.

Sister McCrandle glanced up and seeing them staring, looked meaningfully at them both.

'Now we're for it!' said Mark, moving away.

Bella went with him. 'She's not too bad. Compared to Sister Killeen, she's all sweetness and light.'

'I'm not so sure.'

Eyes blazing, Sister McCrandle stepped out of the sideward.

'Into my office - both of you!'

'Yes, Sister McCrandle,' they chorused.

They did as they were told and waited in her office. Even Bella was afraid now. They felt like schoolchildren about to be punished by the headteacher.

They waited for a long time which made them even more nervous. When the door finally opened, however, it wasn't Sister McCrandle who came in. It was Gilbert Buchanan.

'Which one of you is Bella Denton?' he said.

His broad grin put them at their ease. They both smiled.

'You have my gratitude, young lady.'

'Thank you, sir.'

'I hate to lose patients,' he said, stroking his beard. 'Bad for my reputation. You kept it intact for me.'

'I only did what I had to, Mr Buchanan.'

'You were very observant, Bella. Inquisitive, as well. That's no bad thing. Curiosity is a virtue in a nurse. And you probably saved a man's life into the bargain.' He sighed. 'Not that Mr Devlin will thank you for it, I fear.'

'Why does he want to die?'

'Your guess is as good as mine. My worry is that he may try again. I'm only a surgeon. I patched his body up. I can't do anything for his mind. I leave that to the shrinks.' He smiled at them. 'And to Bella. Just seeing her face would be a tonic for any young man. Keep an eye on Mr Devlin for me, will you?'

He gave Bella a congratulatory pat on the shoulder.

Bella beamed proudly.

CHAPTER ELEVEN

Gordy lunged across the court and stuck out his racket. The squash ball bounced off it and landed just above the tin on the back wall. Karlene darted forward but she had no chance of reaching it in time. The ball died on her and rolled across the wooden floor.

It was a fluke shot but it won the match. Gordy collapsed with exhaustion and sat with his back to the door. Perspiration was streaming off him.

'Another game?' said Karlene, breathing hard.

'No thanks,' he gasped.

'But I'm just getting the hang of it.'

'That's the trouble, Kar!'

The squash court was in the basement of the medical school. Students could book it for a small charge. Karlene had never played before coming to the hospital but showed a keen interest. Gordy offered to teach her and now he was beginning to regret it.

'You improve enormously each time we play,' he complained.

'Isn't that the idea?'

'You're a natural, Kar.'

'I've always liked sport.'

'Give it another month and you'll be teaching *me*!'

She grinned at the compliment and came over to crouch beside him.

'I'm not that good,' she said, modestly. 'I thought I was really off form today. I'm so tired after all those late nights.'

'Then I'd hate to play you when you're really fit. You made me fight for every point.' He used a forearm to wipe the sweat from his forehead. 'Will you be going across to the Burns Unit again this evening?'

'No, not tonight.'

'Isn't Janie going to see her mother?'

'Yes,' said Karlene, 'but she doesn't want to see me.'

'Why not? You've carried her through this crisis.'

'Janie doesn't see it quite that way.'

'What happened?'

Karlene shrugged. 'I made a bad mistake, Gordy. Frightened her off.'

'Well, I wish you'd tell me what the mistake was. I could use it myself. *I* need to frighten someone off.'

'Not that receptionist, by any chance?'

'Harriet Collins. She never gives up.'

'Invite her to play squash with you.'

'You've got to be joking!' he exclaimed. 'I'd never let her near me when I'm wearing shorts.'

'Why not?'

'Because she thinks I've got sexy legs.'

'You have, Gordy.' She slapped his thigh. 'They're great.'

'Well, Harriet's not going to *see* them again.'

Karlene chuckled. 'What else has she seen?'

'Don't you start on me as well,' he moaned. 'I have enough teasing from Bella.'

'From what I hear, you got your own back on her.'

'I gave her a little scare, that's all.'

'Hanging a skeleton in her wardrobe! If you'd done that to me, I'd have hit you with a squash racket.'

'Bella used her pillow. It still hurt.'

Gordy summoned up all his strength and got to his feet.

'Thanks for the game, Kar,' he said. 'I needed that. It flattened me but it also got rid of all my tension.'

'It's woken me up,' she said, rising to her feet. 'I feel good. So what is the situation with this Harriet?'

'She wants me, I don't want her.'

'But you did once?'

'A long time ago.' He gestured hopelessly. 'Harriet is a nice girl but...I've moved on since then. She doesn't do anything for me now.

'Try seeing it from her side.'

'She's obsessed with me. That's her side in a nutshell.'

'Then you've got a problem.'

'What would *you* do?' he asked. 'If a boy persisted in chasing you?'

'Tell him the truth. "I'm just NOT interested".'

'And if that failed?'

'Then I'd show him he was wasting his time.'

'But how, Kar?'

'In the simplest way,' she said. 'I'd get rid of one boyfriend by going out with another.'

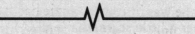

Suzie flicked through the magazine with mounting irritation. All the models were so slim and graceful. They wore fabulous dresses and silk underwear, and were photographed against exotic backgrounds. The message was painful for Suzie.

Slim is beautiful.

She'd always had a good figure but, in her eyes, she was no longer as sylph-like as she had been. The irony was that her weight had actually gone down slightly. When she got on the bathroom scales, she seemed to have shed a few pounds. Yet she was still unhappy about her body. One thing was certain. She would never get on to the pages of a glossy magazine. She hurled it away from her.

She saw two familiar figures go past the window and quickly got up from the sofa. When Mark and Bella came into the living room, Suzie was clattering about in the kitchen. The radio was playing loud music.

'We're back!' called Bella.

'Be there in a tick!' shouted Suzie.

'What a fantastic experience!' said Mark, falling into an armchair. 'I actually spoke to Gilbert Buchanan.'

'*We* spoke to him,' reminded Bella. 'And I was

the one who got the pat on the back.'

'It was wonderful!'

'What was?' said Suzie, coming into the room.

They told her about their day in Marlborough Ward and she was intrigued. Suzie had had a rather dull time, going to lectures and writing up her notes. She envied their involvement in the real life of the hospital.

'Who's turn to make the food?' said Bella.

'Mine,' said Suzie. 'Pasta and Dolmio sauce.'

'OK with me.'

'It'll have to be, Bella. It's all there is. We'll have to go to the supermarket tomorrow.'

'I'll do the shopping,' volunteered Mark.

'Leave it to me,' insisted Suzie. 'I like it.'

'We'll go together, Suzie.'

'No, no. I'll be fine on my own.' She perched on the arm of the sofa. 'I won't start the meal until Gordy and Karlene get back. They've been playing squash.'

'I hope she kills him!' said Bella.

'Go easy on old Gordy,' suggested Mark.

'Yes,' agreed Suzie. 'Time to call a truce.'

'Only when I've won the battle,' said Bella.

'But you won't win,' argued Suzie. 'All you'll do is drag it out. And while you and Gordy are fighting, Karlene, Mark and I all get caught in the crossfire.'

'Then you'll have to learn to duck.'

'Bella!'

'You saw what he did to me with that skeleton.'

'It was a bit scary,' conceded Mark.

'It was malicious.'

'No, it wasn't, Bella,' said Suzie, seriously. 'It was meant to be a joke - it was stupid perhaps and Gordy deserved to get bashed with that pillow. But it's all over now. Put it behind you.'

Bella folded her arms and glared.'I can't.'

Suzie changed the subject.

'I had a long chat with Karlene today. About her friend.'

'Janie?' said Mark.

'Yes. Karlene's got a bit of a problem with her. I'll let her give you the details herself. But what it comes down to is that Janie's cracking under the strain.'

'Who wouldn't?' said Bella with sympathy. 'Her home destroyed. Her father killed. Her mother and kid brother burned in the fire. Any one of those things would be bad enough. Put them all together and it's mind-blowing.'

'That's right,' said Suzie.' Everything in her life has suddenly fallen to pieces. The poor girl must be bewildered.'

Mark pushed his glasses up the bridge of his nose.

'Janie's got a lot of adjustments to make,' he said. 'Especially where her brother's concerned. Vance will never look the same again. They're going to have to build him an entirely new face. Bit by bit.'

'It's amazing what they can do these days,' said

Bella. 'Plastic surgery can disguise the worst of the scars.'

'Yes,' said Mark. 'But not all of them.'

'I'd hate to be in that situation,' said Bella with a shiver. 'It'd be so terrible to have something happen to your face. And I'd hate an injury to my body - don't you agree, Suzie? It'd be horrendous and I'd lose all my confidence.'

'I agree!' said Suzie with feeling, wishing that her own body was as slim and graceful as Bella's.

'Clever make-up can conceal even the worst blemishes,' observed Mark. 'There are cosmetics for men as well as for women. Then there are wigs, of course.'

'Wigs?' repeated Bella.

'According to Karlene, they have quite a collection over at the Burns Unit. They show the patients how effective a good wig can be. It can hide some disfigurements and still look quite natural.'

'It's true,' said Suzie. 'But Vance can hardly wear a wig.'

'Pity!' sighed Mark. 'It might have given him a lot of confidence, to appear more normal to the outside world. A really good wig can fool almost anybody.'

'Yes,' said Bella, excitedly. 'You're right. It can!' And she began to laugh hysterically.

———————⋀———————

Vance was having a different dream this time.

It was a sunny afternoon. He and Janie had taken Coco to the park. The puppy was scampering about on the grass. They were having great fun trying to catch it. Coco dodged them time and again, running through Vance's legs and jumping through Janie's arms. He yelped happily.

Vance was so proud of his little pet. The puppy scurried off towards some bushes and dived into the undergrowth to hide. But his yapping turned to a terrified bark as the bushes suddenly caught fire. The dog was trapped. Vance rushed to save him but the flames were far too high. Yellow tongues licked at him. He felt a searing pain. Smoke began to choke him. The heat was blinding him.

Vance opened his eyes and was dazzled by bright light. He thought at first he was still caught in the fire but the agony seemed to have gone. He narrowed his eyelids. The light gradually dimmed. He could make out shapes.

A face came into view. It was bandaged like his own but he would know those loving eyes anywhere. It was his mother. He was alarmed at her injuries but overjoyed to see her.

'Hello, Vance love,' she said. 'I hoped you'd wake up.'

He was desperate to speak but the words wouldn't come out.

'Don't say anything,' she soothed. 'We'll just be together for a while. Janie sends her love. They'll let her visit you soon. When they think you're up to it.'

She saw his distress and did her best to calm him.

'Yes, I know it's hard, Vance. I know it's lonely. I know it's painful. But you're not ready to go home yet. They'll look after you properly in here. They'll help you. Like they helped me.' She leant close to his face. 'I'll be here every day from now on. You'll see me whenever you want.'

The nightmare was over. Vance smiled inwardly.

———————⎯⋀⎯———————

'You go first,' he urged. 'To see if the coast is clear.'

'Don't be silly.'

'She might be lying in wait out there.'

'That's your problem, not mine.'

'Karlene!'

'I've told you what I'd do. Now, come on.'

Karlene and Gordy had both had a shower after their squash game. But as they were about to leave the medical school. Gordy grew anxious. He was convinced that Harriet was lurking in the shadows, waiting for him.

'Could I ask you a very big favour, Karlene?'

'You can *ask* it,' she said, 'but I'm not promising anything. What do you want?'

'To hold your hand.'

'Not a chance!'

'Only while we cross the car park.'

'No, Gordy.'

'But it was your idea. Use a decoy, you said.'

'All I told you was what *I'd* do in the same situation. That didn't mean I was offering to help you do it.'

'It wouldn't hurt for two minutes.'

'Of course, it would!' said Karlene. 'If Harriet sees us walking hand in hand, she'll think I'm your girlfriend.'

'Exactly!'

'But if any of *my* friends see me, I lose my street cred.'

'I thought you'd be flattered.'

Karlene didn't know whether to laugh or be angry.

'Do me a favour!'

'It won't commit you to anything.'

'No, Gordy,' she said, firmly. 'Forget it. I'll share the house with you. I'll cook for you from time to time. I'll even play squash with you. But that's it! No holding hands.'

'What if Harriet is out there?'

'I'll tell her what an idiot she is, moping after you when she could find herself a real man.'

'I *am* a real man!' he retaliated.

'Then why are you behaving like a mouse?'

'I'm taking sensible precautions, that's all.'

'Find another hand to hold. Mine's not available.'

Karlene picked up her sports bag and sauntered to the door. Gordy scurried behind her. When they came out of the building, they saw the main block towering up into the evening sky. Karlene walked briskly across the car park. Using her as a shield, Gordy kept half a pace behind her.

'Harriet's probably gone home by now,' she said.

'I can't take any chances.'

'She's got better things to do than hang around after work for you.' She pointed towards the main entrance. 'Look, Gordy. Nobody's coming out. You're quite safe.'

He stepped out from behind her. At that moment, the door opened and a female figure came running out of the building.

'No!' he yelled. 'Not again! Please! *Please*!'

He held his bag in front of his face to hide from the ambush but it wasn't Harriet. The girl running towards them hadn't been waiting for him.

It was Janie Palmer.

'Hi Karlene,' she said, rather timidly.

'Oh Janie, good to see you again,' said Karlene, warmly. 'This is a friend of mine - Gordy Robbins.'

Gordy lowered his bag and nodded at Janie. She didn't even look at him.

'I need to talk to you, Karlene. Alone.'

The Caribbean Club was in full swing. Reggae music was playing against a hum of happy voices and laughter. There was a riot of laughter. The main hall was set aside for the youth club. The dartboards and table tennis and pool tables were all occupied. The bar was at the rear of the premises. Nobody under age was allowed in there. It was a place for families - the children going to the youth club while their parents enjoyed a drink with friends.

Janie was in the middle of a throng of people. Everyone wanted to ask after her mother and brother. Madge waddled across in her fur-lined slippers.

'Give the girl some air,' she said, waving away the well-wishers. 'Hello, Janie. Lovely to see you.'

'Hi, Madge.'

'We need a quiet corner,' said Karlene.

'In this place?' Madge gave her rich laugh. 'You asking the impossible. Come on. I'll do the best I can.'

She led them to a table in the coffee bar that was tucked behind a potted palm. The noise was minimised. As they sat down, Karlene took out her purse.

'Two coffees, please.'

'Put your money away,' said Madge. 'These are on the club. We'll even throw in a cake each.'

'Thanks, Madge,' said Janie. 'And thanks for those cards you sent. Mum was very touched.'

'That's the least we could do, child.'

Madge ambled off behind the counter to leave them alone. Karlene kept the talk neutral. She'd brought Janie to the club on purpose. Its warmth and familiarity helped her to relax. The Caribbean Club was one of the few things in her life that hadn't been affected by the fire.

It was also the place where Karlene and Janie had first met. They slowly fell back into their old routine. When the coffees and cakes arrived, they were gossiping and even sharing jokes.

Janie eventually worked her way round to an apology.

'I'm sorry, Karlene.'

'For what?'

'Running away like that.'

'It was my fault.'

'No, you were only trying to help.'

'But in the wrong way.'

'I shouldn't have charged off.'

'Why did you, Janie?'

She fell silent stirring her coffee and staring into it. Karlene didn't rush her. She wasn't going to put the slightest pressure on Janie this time.

'I couldn't take it any more,' said her friend.

'That's understandable.'

'You don't know what it's like. Having Mum and Vance in hospital is bad enough. Especially when they're both so...' Her voice was bitter.

'Being at Aunty Linda's is terrible. Like a prison. I can't breathe in there. They watch me every moment. Aunty Linda nags me all day long.'

'What about your uncle?'

'He's the same,' she said. 'In some ways, Uncle Denzil is worse. I know it's not his fault but he reminds me of...'

She sipped her coffee to ward off tears. Karlene knew what she was going to say. Denzil Naylor was her mother's elder brother. But he had a strange resemblance to Greg Palmer. Every time Janie looked at her uncle, she saw her dead father.

'When are they letting your mum out?' said Karlene.

'Tomorrow afternoon.'

'Well, that's something to look forward to, isn't it?'

'Yes and no.'

'You'd rather have her at home, surely?'

'It's not home, Karlene. It's Aunty Linda's house and there just isn't room for all of us. I'll have to share with my two cousins. Three of us in a small room.'

'Only for a short while, Janie.'

'It'll be hell!'

'Where else can your mum go?'

'Nowhere, really.'

'It's really tough, but you'll have to make the best of it,' said Karlene, gently.

Janie nodded. She seemed to be on the verge of taking Karlene into her confidence but she drew back. Karlene waited patiently.

'Did you see our house?' muttered Janie.

'Yes.'

'We lost everything. Furniture, clothes, everything.'

'I know, it's dreadful.'

'It's not fair, Karlene. It's just not fair!' Silent tears coursed down her face. She brushed them away. 'I keep thinking about Dad. Going back in there to get Coco. Then the two of them getting cut off by the flames. It's terrible!'

Karlene put a hand on her arm. Janie was still crying.

'Why did they have to die, Karlene?'

'They were just unlucky.'

'It would've been different if I'd been there.'

'Janie...'

'No, it would,' said the girl. 'I've worked it out. Dad came looking for me at ten-thirty. If I'd been here in the club, we'd have walked home together and got there just as the fire was starting.'

'Don't torment yourself.'

'Because Dad searched for me, he got back later.'

'You're only guessing that.'

'I'm to blame, Karlene. Don't you see?'

'No, I don't.'

'I'll never forgive myself.'

'You must, Janie,' said Karlene, firmly. 'You might just as well say that your dad was to blame for letting you go out in the first place. Or your mum for taking a bath while the fire got a hold on the kitchen.' Karlene leant over to her. 'Or your brother, even. If Vance hadn't smuggled Coco up to his room, your dad wouldn't have had to go back inside the house. Would he?'

A long pause. 'I suppose not.'

'Do you know whose fault it *really* was, Janie?' She shook her head, sadly.

'The electrician's.'

'What do you mean?'

'That's what caused the fire. Your Aunty Linda told me. It was dodgy wiring in the kitchen. The police thought it might be arson at first but the inspector ruled that out when he searched through the house. It was definitely the faulty wiring, Janie.' She raised her voice slightly for emphasis. '*Not* you staying out later than you should have. Not you at all, in fact. If anyone's to blame, it's that electrician.'

Janie thought it over and a weight seemed to fall slowly from her shoulders. She gave a tentative smile.

'I'm really glad I saw you this evening.'

Karlene grinned. 'Eat your cake.'

'That was very welcome!' said Gordy, pushing his plate aside. 'Nothing like a game of squash for working up an appetite!'

He was in the kitchen with Bella and Mark. They were still buzzing with excitement after their day helping out in Marlborough Ward.

Bella saw the chance to put Gordy down.

'Have *you* ever met Gilbert Buchanan?' she said.

'Not face to face,' said Gordy. 'But he gave us a lecture once. He was hilarious.'

'We were actually alone with him.'

'Stop boasting,' warned Mark.

'I'm entitled to boast,' she said. 'Doctors are not the only people who matter in hospitals. Even a student nurse can help to save a life if she keeps her eyes open.'

'Give her a medal!' said Gordy.

'No need to be sarcastic. You're only jealous.'

'Of what?'

'Me,' she said. 'I rescued a patient. All you've done today is play hide-and-seek with Harriet.'

Gordy winced. 'Stop her, Mark, please,' he said, wearily. 'I'm not in the mood for another argument.'

'Who's arguing?' asked Bella.

'You are,' said Mark, suddenly angry. 'You're just trying to needle him. I was more pleased than you to meet Gilbert Buchanan but I'm not shoving it down Gordy's throat.'

Bella stopped - Mark rarely raised his voice. His words had a sobering effect on her. She looked across at the sink.

'My turn to do the washing up, I think.'

'I'll dry,' offered Mark, getting up from the table. 'The bin needs emptying first. I'll do that as well.'

He pulled the bin from under the sink and lifted out the black plastic liner. He was just about to tie it up when he spotted some things inside it. He'd traced the missing apricot jam.

It was something else that really puzzled him.

'Have either of you been buying Jaffa Cakes?'

'Not me,' said Gordy.

'Can't afford them,' said Bella.

'There're four packets in here.'

He moved them aside with his hand and saw the discarded wrappers from a dozen Mars bars. Mark was baffled. Tying up the end of the plastic bin liner, he took it out into the little garden behind the house and dropped it into the dustbin.

Gordy and Bella were chatting pleasantly when Mark came back in. He was relieved. After fitting a new plastic liner in the bin, he went upstairs. Mark wanted to see if Suzie could throw any light on the mystery. But when he tapped on her door, it swung open. The room was empty.

A noise from the bathroom attracted his attention. It was very distinct and he felt alarmed. Mark was not at all sure what to do.

Suzie was being violently sick.

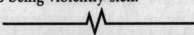

The house in Cameron Street looked more desolate that ever. Its walls were blackened by the fire, its upstairs windows gaped like empty eye-sockets. It was difficult to believe that a family had once lived in such a ruin.

Janie looked at the charred remains of a ladder.

'Dad never had a chance,' she said, sadly.

'No,' said Karlene. 'But he couldn't just leave Coco in there. He borrowed that ladder from a neighbour and climbed back into the house.'

They'd left the Caribbean Club. It had drawn them back together again but it was not the place for an intimate conversation. When Janie asked to go to the house, Karlene agreed. They were standing completely alone in the street.

Karlene felt a surge of anger when she remembered the horrors inflicted on the night of the fire. There had to be some sort of compensation for them.

'Mrs Naylor says you rented the house, Janie.'

'That's right.'

'Who does it belong to?'

'Mr Yates,' said Janie. 'He owns a lot of houses round here. He's a nasty man. Dad used to hate him because he wouldn't pay for any repairs. If something broke, you just had to put up with it. Dad even tried to buy the house off him once but Mr Yates wouldn't hear of it.'

'Didn't you have some sort of contract with him?'

'Contract?'

'A tenancy agreement,' explained Karlene. 'We've got one for our house. Our landlord made us sign it before we moved in. He wanted to make sure he got his rent.'

'So did Mr Yates!'

'But a landlord has obligations under an agreement as well. He has to keep the place in a state of good repair. Tenants have legal rights, Janie.'

'We didn't.'

'You must have.'

'Not with our landlord,' she sighed. 'Dad used to say he was a real bloodsucker.'

'Has Mr Yates been in touch since the fire?'

'We haven't heard a squeak.'

'He's called in at the hospital, surely?' said Karlene. 'I mean, this is his property. His tenants were caught in a fire here. He must be concerned about you.'

'All he thought about was his rent, Karlene.'

'What's his other name?'

'Bernard. Bernard Yates.'

'Does anyone else at the club rent a house from him?'

'Lots of people. Madge is one of them.'

Karlene made a mental note to speak to Madge. She and Janie turned to walk away. It had been a painful visit but it seemed to have broken down some of the barriers that Janie had set up around herself. Karlene sensed that her friend was about to confide in her.

Janie stared at the pavement as they walked.

'You were right,' she admitted.

'Right about what?'

'The night of the fire. I didn't go to the club. That's why Dad couldn't find me there. I was...

with someone.'

There was a lengthy pause. They walked on. When the words finally came, they gushed out in a torrent.

'His name is Alex,' said Janie. 'He goes to my school. I love him, Karlene. He's wonderful. We've been seeing each other for weeks but only in secret. Nobody else knows. I didn't dare tell Dad. He wouldn't have liked Alex at all. He'd have tried to break us up. Dad said I was much too young to have boyfriends.' She stopped and turned to face Karlene. 'That's where I was that night. With Alex. I didn't notice how late it was. So I ran all the way home. Dad would've murdered me!'

'Now I can see why you felt so guilty, Janie.'

'I lied to Mum and Dad,' said her friend. 'I'd been doing it for weeks so that I could be with Alex. Then the fire happened. It was like I was being paid back. I thought someone had done it on purpose. Set fire to the house because of... me and Alex. A sort of warning. That's why I thought I was to blame.'

'But you weren't even in the house.'

'That only made it worse, Karlene. I was the target but they were the victims. I'd *caused* Dad's death. Or that's what it seemed like. I felt like a murderer.'

'Do you feel better now?'

'A little.'

Karlene remembered her earlier talk with Janie's aunt.

'Is that where you went last night, Janie?'

'Did Aunty Linda tell you about that?'

'She and your uncle were very upset.'

'They were vicious to me! They gave me a right telling off!' Janie's bitterness turned to despair. 'He wasn't there, Karlene - the place where we always met. Alex wasn't there.'

'Did he know you were coming?'

'Of course. We had a regular time. He never missed it before. I waited for hours and hours but Alex just didn't turn up. I felt terrible, Karlene.'

Janie clutched her friend in distress.

'I can't bear it if I've lost Alex as well!'

Mark did not have an opportunity to speak to her alone until the following morning. He and Suzie were walking to the hospital together. There was a steady drizzle. They were huddled under her umbrella as they joined the main road. It was a good moment to broach a topic he'd been brooding on.

'Suzie.'

'Yes?'

'Do you know anything about that apricot jam?'

'What jam?'

'We bought a big jar of it,' he said. 'I found it in the bin last night. Empty.'

'Somebody must've eaten it, Mark.'

'The jar was almost full a few days ago.'

'Gordy's the jam maniac. Ask him.'

'He says he didn't touch it.'

'Well, neither did I,' she said, easily. 'You surely didn't think I was the culprit, did you? I don't like jam all that much. I've always preferred honey.'

He let the matter drop. The rain gradually eased off. She lowered her umbrella and shook it out. Mark picked up the subject once more.

'What about those Jaffa Cakes?' he asked.

'Jaffa Cakes?'

'There were four empty boxes in the bin.'

Suzie laughed. 'Mark, what *is* this? Why on earth have you been searching through the rubbish? Are you going to ask me about every item in the bin?'

'Only the Jaffa Cakes.'

'What business is it of yours?'

'It seemed odd, that's all. Four whole packets.'

'Look,' she said, 'if you must know, I finished early yesterday. I had some friends back for tea. A gang of hungry radiographers soon scoffed them.'

'You never mentioned it.'

'I didn't get the chance. I've hardly seen you since.'

'You saw us when we got back from the hospital.'

'I know,' she said, 'but you and Bella wanted to talk about your day in Marlborough Ward.'

'That's true,' he conceded.

'I couldn't get a word in, Mark. Besides, it's hardly front page news. Me having a few friends back for tea. It doesn't compare with you meeting Gilbert Buchanan.'

'No, I suppose not,' he admitted.

She smiled. 'What else was in the rubbish bin?'

'Nothing.'

Mark felt rather foolish. He didn't even bother to ask about the Mars bars. No doubt there was a simple explanation for those as well. But one thing did still worry him and it made him solicitous.

'How are you feeling now, Suzie?'

'Fine.'

'I thought you were off colour the other day.'

'A headache, that's all. Too much studying.'

'What about yesterday evening?'

'Mark, for heaven's sake!'

'I'm interested that's all.'

'I feel terrific, OK? Today *and* yesterday.'

'Sorry.'

'When I want a consultation, I'll go to my GP.'

'Of course...I was just concerned, that's all.'

'No need to be,' she said, giving his arm an affectionate squeeze. 'I'm in good shape. Honestly. Look at me.'

Mark nodded. He was reassured. They went in through the main gate of the hospital. Suzie glanced over her shoulder. Gordy and Karlene were behind them.

'Bella was off early this morning,' she remarked.

'Yeah - crack of dawn.'

'She must love working in the Marlborough Ward.'

'She couldn't wait to see Rob Devlin.'

'Who's that?'

'The patient we told you about. The one who jumped from a train. Bella's taken a real interest in his case. It's got to her somehow. Rob Devlin's only our age you see, and yet he tried to commit suicide in a horrific way. Makes you shiver.'

'It does, Mark. But why is Bella so keen to see him?'

'To make sure he's still alive.'

Rob Devlin was fully conscious now. He was able to piece together what had happened. He remembered feeling in a pit of depression. And the decision to escape from it once and for all. He even remembered the huge gust of wind that hit him as he flung himself from the train. Memory deserted him at that point. He now felt curiously detached from his body. It gave him only distant pain.

He stared at the ceiling. His deep fury had somehow faded away. He was no longer angry with himself for failing in his bid to end it all. He was simply astonished. The chances of surviving the leap from the train were very slim indeed. Yet here he was. Badly injured but still very much alive.

Medication had stabilised him. His problems hadn't gone away but now he took a slightly different view of them. Someone obviously cared for him. He was not as isolated as he'd feared. They'd gone to enormous trouble to save him. He did matter.

The nurse came over to his bed, smiling.

'Good morning, Mr Devlin.'

'Morning,' he murmured.

'How are you feeling today?'

'OK.'

'Good, good. Mr Buchanan will be here soon.'

'Who?'

'The consultant who performed the operation,' she said. 'You had the very best surgeon, Gilbert Buchanan. He'll be so pleased to see that you're back with us.'

Rob's eyelids flickered. His voice was drowsy.
'Wake me...when...he...comes...'

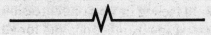

Sister McCrandle kept them hard at it in Marlborough Ward. Bella didn't mind. It was valuable experience and she was getting some fascinating insights. Two new cases had been admitted during the night. Both were students who had cracked under the pressures of university life. Bella was delighted that Rob Devlin was still there. For the first time since he had been in the Critical Care Unit, the nurse monitoring his condition saw slight signs of improvement.

'Take your break now, Bella.'

'Yes, Sister McCrandle.'

'Twenty minutes.'

'I know, Sister McCrandle.'

'Not a moment longer. I'll be waiting.'

It was mid-morning. Ignoring the chance to have a quick cup of coffee, Bella took the lift to the ground floor. She found herself a vantage point in Reception then lifted the pad she'd brought with her. Her pencil was soon busy.

Harriet was unaware of her. She was too preoccupied to notice the student nurse who stood no more than a few yards away. She answered queries, checked appointment cards, dealt with telephone calls. She was extremely busy.

Bella was again struck by how pretty Harriet was. Her shiny fair hair hung down almost to her shoulders. Her upturned nose and the pretty eyes set off her whole face. Bella could only see her in profile at first. She was grateful when another receptionist spoke to Harriet and made her turn round. Bella got a first important glimpse of the back of her head.

A figure in a white coat stepped into her line of vision and leant over the desk. Bella had to abandon her sketch. The young doctor chatted to Harriet. Bella couldn't hear what they said but the receptionist's laugh was loud and clear.

When the figure turned towards her, Bella had a shock. She knew him. It was Damian Holt, one of the junior doctors at the hospital. A tall, rangy Australian, he'd caught her eye during her first week there and she'd made sure she was introduced to him. She'd even gone out with him a couple of times. Bella waved and Damian grinned amiably. He came over and they chatted happily for a few minutes. Clearly he still liked her as much as she liked him. Damian always looked so hunky; he had great eyes and thick, wavy hair. Bella was sorry when he had to go back to Casualty.

She watched him leave then continued her task. She'd almost finished when she realised that Harriet was staring at her.

'What are you doing?' asked the receptionist.

'Mm...nothing,' said Bella, tucking her pad under her arm.

'Can I help you in any way?'

'Yes, I'm trying to find Marlborough Ward.'

'I'm new here myself,' said Harriet, 'but I've got a diagram of the hospital somewhere.' She looked down at her desk. 'Ah, here it is. You'll find Marlborough Ward on the...now, let me see, where are we...yes, on the third floor in the East Wing. OK?'

Harriet glanced up - but Bella had vanished.

'You sure you wouldn't like anything, Karlene?' said Madge.

'No, thanks. This is a flying visit.'

'You lucky to find me. I was checking my stock.'

'Then I won't interrupt you for long.'

'I work and talk at the same time,' said the old woman. 'Hey, wasn't it lovely to see Janie here again last night.'

'That's why I came, Madge. She needs help.'

'That whole family does.'

Karlene had sacrificed her lunch hour to hurry round to the Caribbean Club. Still in her trusty slippers, Madge was going along checking her shelves in the coffee bar and making notes on a scrap of paper.

'More sausage rolls,' she said to herself. 'Three dozen.'

'I believe you know Bernard Yates.'

Madge made a face. 'I know him. My landlord.'

'What sort of man is he, Madge?'

'The worst kind, Karlene. Out to make as much money as he can in the quickest possible way. He walks all over us. If we could afford to live anywhere else, we would.'

'He owned the Palmer house as well, didn't he?'

'Don't I know it!' said Madge. 'Me and Greg Palmer sat in this coffee bar many times and swapped stories about Mr Yates. Don't know which of us despised that man the most.'

'Did you sign a tenancy agreement with him?'

'My husband did.'

'Does it require the landlord to maintain the property in a good state of repair?'

'Oh, yes!' said Madge, hooting with derisive laughter. 'But he only comes near us when he wants the rent. The place has to be falling down around us before he'll do anything.'

'That's what Janie said.'

'We all in the same boat, Karlene.'

'Where does this Mr Yates live?'

'Some posh house out in the country. He's a very rich man. Into all this B and B as well, you see.'

'Bed and breakfast?'

'Yes, Karlene,' said Madge, peering into a huge tin of coffee. 'When they do up Council houses, they move tenants out into temporary accommodation. Cheap hotels that do B and B. Mr Yates has dozens. They only big houses with a fancy name stuck across the front. But he calls them hotels.'

'Do you know where any of them are?'

'One or two.' Madge looked up in alarm. 'But you don't want to go staying in them places, Karlene. They got fleas.'

'Just give me the names,' said Karlene, taking out a notebook and a biro. 'And while we're at it, tell me if there's anybody else at the club who rents their house from him. Especially people with complaints.'

'They *all* got complaints.'

'Let's start with the hotels, shall we?'

Madge folded her arms and rested them on the counter.

'They not hotels, Karlene. They fire-traps.'

———————/\/———————

The taxi pulled into Cameron Street and stopped outside the shell of the Palmer House. Sad eyes peered out from behind a pair of dark glasses. Diane Palmer had recovered from smoke inhalation and suffered relatively minor burns. Released from hospital that afternoon, she insisted on being driven to her house in the taxi. She wanted to remind herself of what she'd lost.

Linda Naylor and Janie sat in the back of the taxi with her, careful not to rub against her injuries in any way.

'Don't look, Mum, said Janie. 'It'll upset you.'

'I'm all right.'

'They had vandals in there next morning,' said

her sister-in-law, 'so they boarded it up. Some people got no respect. This area goes down and down. I wouldn't have been surprised if it *had* been arson. I've seen those gangs on street corners.'

Mrs Palmer let nostalgia soothe her for a moment. She tried to recall the house when it was at its best, full of life and laughter. She and her husband had raised their little family there. They'd shared so many wonderful times within its walls. With all its faults, it had been their home.

'Remember what they told you,' said Janie, plaintively. 'You've got to rest as much as possible.'

'I know.'

'Your room is all ready for you, Diane,' said Linda. 'We've moved Janie in with the girls so that you can be on your own. It's small but clean.'

'Thank you, Linda.'

'God knows what we'll do when Vance comes out of hospital! There's no way we can fit him in as well.'

'We'll have moved by then,' said Janie, hopefully.

'Where to?' challenged her aunt.

'Anywhere! Anywhere to get away from you,' she muttered under her breath.

'And where's the money going to come from for that?'

'Let's take it one step at the time,' said Mrs Palmer, still staring through the window. 'It's all happened so quickly. My head is in a whirl. I'm taking each day as it comes.'

Linda made clucking sounds of sympathy.

'Shall we make a move, then?'

'One last look,' said Mrs Palmer. 'That's all.'

She heaved a sigh. The house was in a far worse state than she'd imagined. That phase of her life was well and truly over. They'd have to start afresh.

Her burns were smarting badly but the pain in her heart was far deeper. Her husband was dead and her son was still seriously ill in hospital. It was not just a home that had been destroyed. She was looking out at a lifetime that had gone up in smoke.

'Thank you, driver,' she said, quietly. 'We can go now.'

CHAPTER FOURTEEN

It was his turn to lie in wait and pounce.

'I need to speak to you for a few minutes, Harriet.'

'Gordy!' she exclaimed in delight.

'Can we go somewhere?'

'Of course - anywhere!'

'Let's go through here. At least it'll be private.'

Gordy Robbins lifted the bar on the emergency exit and pushed the metal door open. They stood at the top of a flight of stone steps. It was mid-afternoon and he'd intercepted her as she left the canteen after her break. Gordy had a determined glint in his eye.

Harriet was more interested in the smell of his breath.

'You've been drinking,' she chastised.

'I only had one or two.'

'You stink of whisky.'

'Don't distract me. I've been working up to this.'

He took her purposefully by the shoulders but she thought he was trying to kiss her. She melted into his arms with a willing smile on her upturned face.

'This is wonderful, Gordy. You're so impulsive!'

'Stand up straight,' he ordered.

'Kiss me! Like you did in that tent.'

'Once and for all, forget the flaming tent!' he yelled.

His intensity made her take a step back, blinking.

'We can't go on like this, Harriet,' he said. 'It's ruining my life. There I was this morning, listening to an anatomy lecture, and all I could think about was you.'

'That's beautiful!' she said, dreamily.

'It was a disaster. I didn't hear a word. When I was asked a question by the lecturer, I made a complete idiot of myself.' He pointed at her. 'All because of you!'

'But, Gordy,' she said, 'you're always in *my* thoughts.'

'It's got to stop, Harriet.'

'Stop?'

'I'm fed up with hiding. I'm fed up with looking over my shoulder all the time. I'm fed up with all the deceit.'

'Then let's end it right now, darling.'

His spirits rose. 'You mean that?'

'Of course. We'll get married as soon as possible.'

'No!'

'Wouldn't that solve both our problems?'

'Harriet,' he said, taking a deep breath and trying to control his emotions. 'You're a lovely girl. I'll always want us to be friends. But I can never - never in a million years - become your husband.'

She smiled softly. 'I expected this to happen.'

'What..?'

'Your attack of cold feet. I undertstand.'

'What are you on about?'

'An article I read in a magazine. About how guys always panic at the last moment. The idea of marriage frightens them. They worry about losing their manhood.'

'You're dead right!'

'But they usually come through that phase.'

'It's not a phase, Harriet.'

'I'll be here when you change your mind again,' she said, calmly. 'Go off and do your own thing then come back to me.' She kissed him on the cheek. 'Only do it before the end of the month. I need you back in place by then.'

'Why?'

'My father wants to meet you. He's sales manager for a pharmaceutical company and he's coming to this area.' She linked arms with him and stood proudly by his side. 'Daddy's so keen to meet his future son-in-law.'

Gordy was defeated again.

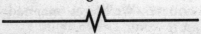

Bella had never worked so hard - her second day in Marlborough Ward was one of the best and most instructive days she'd ever had at the hospital, and the most rewarding. Sister McCrandle supervised her, and the other nurses were really helpful. Having Mark alongside her was another bonus. He had real sympathy for the patients and seemed able to understand them.

The biggest thrill for her was the news that Rob Devlin was out of danger. She peered through the observation window at him and gave an encouraging wave. He was off the life-support machine. He'd come through the critical post-operative period. Now the physical healing could start to take place and Bella hoped his emotional recovery would also begin.

In spite of an onerous day, she still had the energy to leave the hospital at speed. There was so much to do. She reached the department store just in time, found what she needed then ran back to the house at a steady jog

Estimating she only had half an hour alone at most, Bella didn't waste a second of it. Her plan had already been formulated. Now she put it into operation. Her first task was to assemble all the items she needed.

She hit a snag. None of her own dresses would fit. They were too small. Karlene's clothes, on the other hand, were a bit too large. Bella decided to raid Suzie's wardrobe. Suzie would complain loudly but it would be worth it.

'We want you to look your best, old girl, don't we?' she said.

Bella let herself into Suzie's room and opened the wardrobe. A row of dresses confronted her. She took them out one by one to examine them. She decided on the green dress - it was calf-length and had long, slim sleeves.

Bella was just about to hang the other dresses back on the rail when something gleamed up at her from the bottom of the wardrobe. It was the silver wrapping paper on some chocolate teacakes.

She bent down to investigate and found a couple of large boxes. Bella was amazed. Instead of a few, Suzie had a secret horde of five dozen chocolate teacakes.

'How long will it all take, Mr Quentin?' she asked.

'It's impossible to put a time limit on it,' he said. 'Vance is going to need a series of major operations over the next few months but the full treatment may not be completed for some years.'

'Years!'

'Plastic surgery is a slow process.'

Karlene was so grateful to her tutor. Catherine White had arranged for her to meet Donald Quentin so that she could get first-hand information about Vance Palmer. They were in the surgeon's office. When he realised the key role that Karlene had played in the Palmer family tragedy, he was ready to answer many of her questions. Medical ethics would not let him release any confidential information but he was happy to talk in general terms about his work.

'What do the operations entail, Mr Quentin?'

'The initial stage of facial reconstruction is part of the overall programme, Karlene. The object of that is to obtain one hundred per cent skin replacement.'

'How will that be done?'

'Vance suffered full-thickness burns,' he said. 'Skin grafts will be taken from his legs and other unaffected areas. They'll be used to create a whole new face for him.'

'How different will it be?'

'*Very* different. The family must understand that.'

'Vance was such a handsome boy. Especially when he laughed, his whole face lit up. It's awful to think he'll never look anything like that again.'

'Vance must accept that,' he said, gently. 'There are no easy solutions. Lengthy plastic surgery will put him under great strain. Mentally as well as physically.'

'Will he be in much pain?' she asked.

'Far less than patients used to be. They used to dread the regular inspection and dressing of burns. It could be extremely painful at times. Even with saline baths. But now we have new anaesthetising drugs,' he said. 'They numb your senses without knocking you out. You just feel rather drowsy.'

'That's good to hear. I hate the thought of Vance being hurt any more. He's suffered enough as it is.'

'I know,' Mr Quentin said, sympathetically.

'How many operations will there be?'

He shrugged. 'That depends, Karlene. Patients need a lot of stamina to withstand intensive treatment. Vance is a sturdy lad but he's still young. We'll have to go very carefully.'

She paused. 'Does he know about his father?'

'Yes. His mother told him. I was with them.'

'What about his puppy?'

'There was no point in keeping it from him any longer,' said Mr Quentin. 'Vance was only tormenting himself about Coco. Now he knows the truth.'

Karlene wished that she'd been there to comfort him.

'When it's all over,' she said, 'and all the plastic surgery is finished, will he be able to lead a normal life?'

'To a great extent. If he can develop the right outlook.'

'In what way, Mr Quentin?'

'Vance will always look rather unusual,' he warned. 'Some people will be afraid of him, others may just look away. Children can be the worst. They just stare. Vance must learn to cope with all those reactions.'

'That will be really hard for him.'

'Yes, Karlene.'

'Vance will lose out on so much.'

'He'll also be very scared of any open fires,' he explained. 'He may jump if someone strikes a match to light a cigarette. The nightmares have already started. He's suffering the ordeal all over again. You can see why he'll shy away from a naked flame.'

'Will Vance ever overcome that fear?'

'In time. With help. But in the short-term, Karlene...'

'No more bonfire nights.'

She got up and thanked him for giving her his time. Karlene had a much clearer idea of what lay ahead for the Palmer family. She knew now how best to help them.

Donald Quentin rose to his feet and opened the door for her. He gave her one last piece of advice.

'Plastic surgery can do amazing things,' he said with a note of pride, 'but it can only heal the scars on the outside. The ones on the *inside* are the deepest. We can't do a thing about those. But you might, Karlene. Good luck.'

———————⋀———————

'I bungled it, Mark,' he said, ruefully. 'Completely bungled it.'

'Have you thought of writing Harriet a letter?'

'If this goes on, I will - a suicide note!'

'Don't joke about things like that, Gordy,' said Mark. 'If you saw those patients in Marlborough Ward, you'd never laugh about suicide.'

They walked home from the hospital together. Gordy was utterly defeated. He confided in Mark but he added a stern warning.

'Don't you dare mention this to Bella!'

'I wouldn't dream of it, Gordy.'

'She'd taunt me all evening. Bella can be so cruel when she wants to be.'

'You do provoke her sometimes.'

'Maybe. Listen, don't say anything to Suzie or to Karlene either. I tried asking for their help and they were both useless. At a time like this, I need to rely on my friends.'

'I won't breathe a word to anyone.'

'Thanks, Mark.'

A new idea struck him. He looked shrewdly at his companion.

'I don't suppose you'd speak to Harriet for me?'

'Me? No way!'

'But I'll tell you exactly what to say.'

'If you knew exactly what to say, you wouldn't be in this mess. Sorry, Gordy. Count me out. I just don't have the magic touch with girls.'

'I'm beginning to wish I didn't.'

'You obviously knew how to turn Harriet on.'

'What I need is to turn her off again!'

Mark shrugged. 'Honesty is the best policy.'

'Not with her. She twists every word I say.'

'Maybe her interest in you will just ebb away.'

'It's coming at me like a tidal wave,' howled Gordy. 'I feel like King Canute. Sitting there and getting soaked.'

Mark tried not to smile. They reached the house and he fumbled for his key. Gordy let out a long sigh of relief.

'Home at last!'

'She won't trouble you here.'

He opened the door and they went into the hall.

'This is the one place I feel safe, Mark. My citadel. Whatever happens, Harriet Collins will never get in here.'

Gordy went into the living room and stopped dead. Through the open door of the kitchen, he could see someone sitting at the table with her back to him. He shuddered and clutched his head. That fair hair was unmistakable.

It was Harriet.

Bella waved to him from the kithen.

'Come on in, Gordy,' she said, cheerily. 'I invited Harriet back for a cup of tea. As a surprise for you.'

Gordy bared his teeth at her and growled but it was Harriet who bore the brunt of his anger. She'd invaded his castle - his place of retreat. He could never forgive her for that.

He charged up to her ready to have it out once and for all.

'I'm sorry, Harriet, but you'll have to go! Now!'

He shook her so hard that her wig fell off - exposing a bald skull. Gordy wasn't holding Harriet at all. He was wrestling with Matilda, his skeleton.

Bella collapsed with giggles at her successful hoax.

'You should see the look on your face!'

CHAPTER FIFTEEN

When Suzie came back, the argument was in full swing.

'That was a rotten trick!' yelled Gordy.

'Look what you did to *me*!' retorted Bella.

'I almost flipped when I saw her sitting there.'

They continued to argue and Suzie had to shout above the noise.

'What's going on?' she demanded.

They fell silent. Suzie saw her dress on the skeleton.

'That's mine!' she said. 'How on earth did it get there?'

'Bella stole it!' said Gordy.

'I only borrowed it.' She was beginning to feel rather guilty.

'You pinched Matilda as well,' Gordy said. 'If there's any damage to her, I'll send you a bill.'

'Shut up, you two!' said Suzie.

Mark explained what had happened. Suzie knew the only way to defuse the situation was to separate Gordy and Bella.

'Take your skeleton upstairs, Gordy,' she suggested. 'But be careful when you remove that dress. Mark will give you a hand.'

Together they lifted Matilda and went out of the room. Suzie was furious. If Bella had been into her wardrobe, she might have seen the food that was hidden there. Suzie tried to control her anger as she rounded on Bella.

'What the hell are you playing at?' she said.

'It was a joke, that's all.'

'Then why aren't we all laughing?'

'You saw what Gordy did to me.'

'Yes,' said Suzie. 'It was stupid and childish. You were right to hit him with a pillow but that should have been the end of it. As for using one of my dresses, Bella, how would you like it if I went poking around in your room?'

Bella was contrite. 'Sorry, but I had to get my own back on Gordy somehow.'

'If you and he can't get on together, then you'll have to leave. Both of you.'

Bella was shocked. 'You'd throw us out?'

'We're not putting up with this nonsense any longer.'

Bella swallowed hard. She'd never seen Suzie so angry. She couldn't understand why her friend was quite so furious about a childish prank. It was scary.

'It won't happen again. I promise,' said Bella with a shrug. 'I just couldn't help it. But it's all over now - we'll bury the hatchet.'

'Prove it.'

'What do you mean?'

'Apologise to Gordy. Make it up with him or out you go.'

Bella was subdued. 'All right, Suzie. I'll try.' She looked up. 'But he's in this as well. I'm not the only one to blame.'

'No,' agreed Suzie. 'I'll speak to Gordy, don't worry.'

'Will you tell him what you just told me?'

'Yes, Bella. Same message. Make friends or make tracks.'

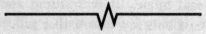

Karlene had walked and talked for hours. She was glad to be able to relax in the coffee bar at the Caribbean Club.

'Thanks for coming to fetch me,' said Janie.

'I wanted to see how you're getting on. Your mother seems to have settled in quite well.'

'She's so pleased to be out of hospital. She'll have to go back regularly to have the dressings changed, but they'll send an ambulance.'

'It must be great to have her back home again.'

'Only it's not our home, Karlene.'

It was a quiet night at the club. A few of the other tables were occupied. Madge was washing up cups in the sink behind the counter.

'I spoke to Mr Quentin today,' said Karlene.

'The plastic surgeon? What did he say?'

'Lots of things, Janie. It's one of the reasons I wanted to see you. He told me that Vance knows about your Dad.'

Janie lowered her head. 'Yes.'

'When's the funeral?'

'The day after tomorrow. At two o'clock. It was delayed until Mum was well enough to go.'

'I'll be there as well.'

Janie was touched. 'Thank you, Karlene. That'll help us all.'

Madge came shuffling over to collect their empty cups.

'You been busy today, Karlene,' she said with a chuckle.

'I knocked on a few doors, that's all.'

'A few! Six or seven people told me you called on them.'

'I was collecting horror stories about Bernard Yates.'

'Mr Yates!' said Janie. 'Our landlord?'

'That's him, child,' said Madge. 'The old miser.'

She took the cups back to the sink and started singing.

'Why were you asking about Mr Yates?' asked Janie.

'Because he was responsible for the fire. Indirectly.'

'You'd never prove that. He'll wriggle out of it.'

'I'm not so sure. That didn't happen last time. Bernard Yates has been prosecuted twice before. On both occasions he was fined - for breaking fire regulations. The most recent case was six months ago. He owns a small hotel called The Regent. I went to see it - it's a disgusting place. He's got eight families crammed in it, and it had had no fire precautions at all.'

'How did they catch him?'

'Just a random call from an inspector. It was a second offence so the fine was heavy. And they made him pay to bring everything up to standard. He had to put in smoke alarms, fire extinguishers and an emergency exit.' She tapped her bag. 'It's all written down in here, Janie. Along with reports from his other tenants.'

'What will you do with it?'

'I rang a solicitor,' said Karlene, 'and he was very encouraging. I'm going to show him all the evidence when I've finished. He wouldn't commit himself over the phone, of course, but he said that it sounded as if we had a very good case. Bernard Yates is a criminal.' She grinned. 'We'll get him.'

'Then maybe there'll be money coming to us?' said Janie, hopefully.

'With luck - in time.'

'Thanks, Karlene. You're a real friend.'

She was delighted to see the trace of a smile on Janie's face again.

'Talking of friends,' she said. 'Any sign of Alex?'

The smile vanished. 'None.'

'Have you been round to his house?'

'I couldn't do that!' said Janie in alarm.

'Why not?'

'I told you. We've had to keep it secret.'

'Ring him up. Ask him where he's been.'

'He's not on the phone.'

'See him at school, then.'

'I haven't been since the fire.' Janie was close to tears. 'I'm afraid he's gone off me, Karlene. I couldn't take that. I'm scared Alex has lost interest in me.'

'I'm sure he hasn't. He cares about you. He's probably desperate for news of you. Why not write to him, or else wait and talk when you see him back at school.' Karlene glanced around. 'Better still, come here on Friday night. Most of the kids in the area will turn up.'

'Not Alex.'

'Isn't he a member?'

'No,' said Janie. 'He'd be a bit out of place. He's white.' She smiled sadly. 'Now you see why I thought that fire was my fault. I was afraid that someone had found out about us and hit out at me. You know how vicious some people can be when they see a black girl with a white boyfriend.'

'Oh yes,' said Karlene with feeling. 'I know.'

———⋀———

Mark was lying on the sofa watching a late film on television. The house was peaceful at last. Gordy and Bella had calmed down after Suzie's words. They kept out of each other's way all evening and went to bed early.

As the film ended and the credits rolled, Mark thought he heard creaking in the passageway. He switched off the television, straining his ears. There was a metallic click, as though someone had just left the house.

Mark was puzzled. It was past midnight. He went to the front door and looked out. It was pitch dark. He couldn't at first pick out the figure who was moving at speed down the street. When she walked into a pool of light from one of the streetlamps, he recognised Suzie. Wearing a track suit, she was pounding along the pavement. It was not gentle jogging. Suzie was pushing herself really hard. Mark was baffled.

On impulse, he went upstairs and slipped quietly into her room. The bedside lamp was on but most of the room was in shadow. He saw nothing unusual and began to feel guilty for intruding.

Suzie could go for a late-night run if she chose. Why should he worry? As he moved to the door, he caught sight of a plastic bag. It was tucked under the bed and a box protruded from it. Mark took a closer look. He found himself holding an empty chocolate teacake packet.

Other images came into his mind: a large jam jar, four packets of Jaffa cakes, several discarded wrappers from Mars bars. He remembered the sound of Suzie being sick in the bathroom. She wasn't simply out jogging. She needed help.

Mark was already wearing a sweatshirt, jeans and trainers. He collected his jacket from downstairs and went out into the street. He ran after Suzie towards the main road. Fit and lithe, he was confident he would catch up with her. The road was splashed with light. He expected to catch sight of her at any moment.

But there was no sign of her. Mark ran steadily until he reached a point where the road straightened. He could see for almost half a mile ahead. No Suzie. She had either turned into a side-street or kept up a much faster pace than he'd expected.

Looking up and down the road in both directions, he wondered where on earth she could be. The wheezing noise gave him his answer - someone was in pain.

Suzie was in the doorway of a shop. Bent double, she had one hand to her chest and was gasping for air. He sprinted over and put an arm around her.

'Suzie! Are you all right?' he said.

'Feel a bit sick, that's all,' she gasped.

'What are you *doing* out here at this time of night?'

'I just felt like a run.'

Still panting, Suzie stood up and looked at Mark's face. He knew. There was no point in trying to deceive him any longer. Mark not only knew, he cared enough to come out and look for her.

She put both arms on his shoulders for support.

'It was me, Mark,' she confessed.

'Save your breath till you feel better.'

'It was me who ate that apricot jam... and all the other things you found in the bin. I couldn't stop myself.'

'You've hardly eaten any meals with us.'

'That's because I was so ashamed, Mark. Ashamed of the way I look. I'm getting so fat.'

She turned away as a wave of nausea

overwhelmed her. The run wasn't just a form of punishment - she did it to make herself sick. Suzie began to retch. Mark gave her a handkerchief and she held it to her mouth for a moment.

'Thanks,' she said.

'But you look great, Suzie and you're certainly not fat.'

'But I keep putting on weight.'

'That's not true,' he assured her, gently. 'If anything, you've lost too much weight. But you'll soon put it on again if you eat all that chocolate.'

'It cheers me up, Mark.'

'Why do you need cheering up, Suzie?' He was very concerned.

'I don't know.'

She leant back against the shop window and took in deep lungfuls of air. It steadied her slightly.

'It's ridiculous,' she said. 'I starve myself to lose weight then I have these midnight binges. Stuffing myself with jam and chocolates...anything. I was really disgusted with myself tonight. I ate two dozen chocolate cakes. I'd hidden a supply of them in my wardrobe. That's why I was so mad when Suzie took that dress of mine. I was afraid she'd seen them behind my clothes.' She let out a huge sigh of despair. 'Two dozen, Mark! Isn't that revolting?'

'I think it's time you had some real food, Suzie.'

'No! I must lose weight.'

'Suzie, you don't *need* to - you look less attractive, and too frail when you're thin. You need to be healthy - to follow a sensible diet,' he said. 'And if you take regular exercise, there'll be no need to put yourself through this torture.'

'I know...But do I look fat to you, Mark?'

'Just the opposite. You look fine to me. But that's not the point. If you don't feel comfortable about your body, then you must do something about it. Maybe we could exercise together - go jogging, or something, like this?' He smiled at her, trying to make her see that he really did think she looked great and wanted to help her overcome her feelings of inadequacy. 'But seriously, we could go swimming together. There's lots of things we can do. But I can't tell you what food to eat. You need to see a doctor about that. Or a nutritionist.'

'Thanks, Mark. I'm so relieved you know what I've been doing.'

'Could we go somewhere warmer? It's cold out here.'

'Sure.'

They walked arm in arm in the direction of the house.

'Ridiculous, isn't it?' she said. 'I'm being trained to look after people and I'm turning into a patient myself. Thank goodness I had a helpful nurse on hand.' She squeezed his arm. 'You won't tell the others, will you?'

'No, Suzie,' he promised. 'On one condition.'

'What's that?'

'No more midnight binges. Unless I'm invited...OK?'

Gordy was still upset by the hoax Bella had played on him. But when his temper had cooled, he came to see that he was partly to blame for the friction between them. She goaded him so much he had struck back. He should have known that Bella wouldn't let it rest there.

Harriet was the real cause of it all. If she hadn't jumped out of Gordy's past like an unwanted ghost, none of the disruption would have happened. He really had to make a decisive break from her. Harriet was upsetting his entire life.

After having a restless night, thinking of what he should do, he got up early next morning and wrote a letter to Harriet. It was short and blunt but she had left him no option. She refused to listen to him when he did try to speak to her. The words would have more affect down on paper in black and white.

'Morning, Gordy.'

'Hi, Mark.'

'Off already?'

'Yes, I've got an appointment at the hospital.'

'With a doctor, you mean?'

'With a receptionist.'

Gordy was putting on his coat when Mark came down for breakfast. Nobody else was up. Gordy was subdued. He felt embarrassed by the way he'd behaved the night before.

'What are you going to say to Harriet?'

'This.' Gordy held up the letter. 'It's all over.'

'Will she believe you this time?'

'I hope so. She's done enough damage around here.'

He heard someone coming out of the bathroom and made a quick exit. The last person he wanted to meet at that moment was Bella. In fact, it was Suzie who came downstairs.

'Good morning, Mark.'

'How are you today?'

'Much better, thanks.'

'Feel like some grub?'

'I'll make myself some toast in a minute.'

'Good.' He gave her a wink. 'Make some for me at the same time, please.'

After they'd talked far into the night, Suzie promised she would try and take a more positive view of her own self-image. If she began to think she was overweight, diet and exercise would be her watchwords from now on. The remaining chocolate cakes had been thrown uneaten into the bin. There would be no more secret binges.

Mark's help and support would always be there to count on and she felt as though a huge weight had been lifted from her shoulders.

They chatted for a few minutes then heard the clatter of feet on the stairs. Bella came dashing in.

'Where's Gordy?' she asked.

'Gone to the hospital,' said Mark.

'But I had an idea - about Harriet.'

'As long as it doesn't involve borrowing my clothes,' said Suzie, sharply. 'They're not available.'

'I want to help him,' said Bella. 'To make amends.'

'Then you'll have to be quick,' said Mark. 'Gordy has gone to the hospital to have it out with Harriet. If you rush, you might just catch him.'

Bella dashed out of the house without speaking.

'She's had no breakfast,' noted Suzie.

'Then you'll have to eat it for her, won't you?'

Suzie laughed. She felt a sense of release.

------------/\/------------

Harriet was talking to someone when he arrived. Gordy lurked in a corner of Reception and waited. Even at that hour, it was quite busy and people were coming in through the door all the time. Gordy fingered the letter in his pocket and prayed that it would do the trick.

He paid no attention to Harriet's companion until the young man turned around. It was Damian Holt, the junior doctor. He had just arrived for work at the hospital. As they knew each other Gordy gave him a nod in greeting. Damian waved, cheerily.

Harriet was alone now, going through some papers on her desk. She looked calm and untroubled. Guilt made Gordy hesitate for a moment. His letter would definitely hurt her. Then he remembered that her father was coming to the area. Once Gordy met him, he would be involved even more in the Collins' family.

He had to get out before it was too late.

'Here goes!' he said to himself. 'Keep it short and sweet.'

He took out the letter and headed for the counter. Harriet looked up from her papers and smiled at him.

'Gordy! What a lovely surprise!'

'I've got something for you,' he said.

'How nice!'

'Wait until you read it.'

He held out the letter and a hand snatched it from him. It was Bella. She flung her arms around Gordy's neck and kissed him on the lips.

'There you are, darling!'

'Bella!'

'You promised to buy me breakfast.'

'I did?'

'You know you did.' She turned to Harriet. 'Excuse us.'

Harriet just stared in amazement.

'Come on, then,' said Bella, linking arms with him.

'Ah...yes. 'Bye, Harriet.'

'But you said you had something for me.'

'Not any more.'

He and Bella marched into the lift together. When the doors closed, she turned to him with a broad grin.

'Are we friends again, Gordy?'

'You bet!'

'What will he look like, Karlene?' asked Janie.

'He'll look like Vance, your little brother.'

'His face, I meant. Will it be like Mum's?'

'Yes, Janie. Covered with dressings. But try not to stare. Just act as naturally as you can. For Vance's sake.'

'You'll be with me, won't you?'

'All the way,' said Karlene.

Janie was seeing her brother for the first time since the fire. He had undergone some preliminary surgery and been sedated for long periods. But he was more alert now and was asking for his sister.

'I feel so excited,' she said. 'Yet so afraid.'

'This is a big moment for Vance. Do your best to keep his spirits up.'

They went into the side ward. A nurse was chatting to Vance as they came in. She looked up and smiled welcomingly and then left them to be on their own.

'Hello, Vance,' said Janie with a smile.

He managed a guttural noise of greeting.

'You remember my friend, Karlene, don't you?'

'Of course he does,' said Karlene, taking one of the seats beside the bed. 'Hello, Vance. Good to see you again. I spoke to Mr Quentin yesterday. He's really pleased with how you're getting on. He says you're one of his star patients.'

Vance managed an approving noise. He was glad to see Janie.

He was still heavily bandaged and his face was quite unrecognisable beneath the dressing. His cheeks were still swollen and his hair had been shaved close to the skin. An intravenous drip was attached to his left arm.

'Everything's fine,' said Janie, starting to talk too quickly. 'You're not to worry about us. We're staying with Aunty Linda and Uncle Denzil. It's a bit cramped but we manage. Mum'll be in to see you when the ambulance brings her for her check-up. I thought I'd come in first.'

Karlene put a hand on her arm to slow her down.

'All your friends have been asking after you,' said Janie. 'Billy, Keg, Jimsie, Leroy - all of them.'

Karlene looked at the mass of cards on his bedside table.

'Your mum was very jealous, Vance,' she said, winking at him. 'You got more Get Well cards than she did.'

'How are they looking after you in here? OK?'

He managed to nod his head very gently.

'Mr Quentin will take care of you,' said Karlene, soothingly. 'I know you wouldn't choose to be in here but think of the advantages: no school, no homework, no jobs to do around the house. You can just lie around all day and wait for them to feed you.'

Vance made no response. He still looked confused.

'We went down to the club,' said Janie. 'Madge

sends her love. She'll be along to see you before too long.'

'There'll be a queue of us outside your door.'

'Aunty Linda and Uncle Denzil will come, too.'

There was an uneasy pause. Karlene nudged her.

'Oh, yes,' remembered Janie. 'I've brought you a present.' She took a tape from her bag. 'It's Michael Jackson.'

'Mr Quentin said you listened to music on the radio a lot. I've got an old cassette player you can borrow.'

Vance managed to nod his head slightly, to thank them.

'I've got a present for you as well,' Karlene continued, as she took something from her bag. 'Would you like me to open it for you? It looks as if you're pretty tied up at the moment.'

He looked suspiciously at the present. It was covered in bright wrapping paper. Karlene peeled back slowly, making sure that he could see it all the time. When the paper was off, she held the object closer to his face.

It was a small, fluffy dog. She put it on his chest.

'We thought it looked like Coco,' said Janie.

'Keep an eye on him, Vance,' warned Karlene. 'He bites.'

'He'll look after you. Until you come out of hospital. Mum says we can buy a real puppy then.'

They'd got through to him at last. Tears welled

up in Vance's eyes as he struggled to thank them. Janie moved in close, wanting to put her arms around him but knowing that she couldn't because of his injuries. Her own eyes filled with tears. They cried quietly together.

Karlene stole away unseen. She felt they needed to be alone.

———⋀———

'Have you heard the news, Bella? They found someone at last.'

'Who?'

'The police.'

'What are you talking about, Mark?'

'Rob Devlin. In the Critical Care Unit. They've tracked down his family - someone's in there right now.'

Bella and Mark were still on attachment to Marlborough Ward. She was stacking boxes of cotton wool in the storeroom when Mark popped his head in.

'One person or two?' she said.

'One.'

'Male or female?'

'Female.'

'I knew it!' decided Bella. 'It's her. The girlfriend. The one he tried to kill himself over. I always said he jumped from that train when his love life went wrong. I bet it's his old girlfriend. Rushing back to his side.'

'What will you bet?'

'The price of lunch.'

'Then reach for your purse, Bella,' he said. 'Unless Rob Devlin likes older women, that's no girlfriend in there. She must be fifty, if she's a day. I think she's his mother.'

'What a disappointment!'

Bella's curiosity was roused. She went back into the ward and peered through the observation window of the critical care unit. Rob Devlin lay on his bed. Leaning over him with maternal concern was a tall, grey-haired woman in a smart suit. She and Rob were having an intense conversation.

'Girlfriend?' said Mark.

Bella capitulated. 'Mother!'

'See you for lunch.'

Bella went disconsolately back to the storeroom. She had looked in on Rob Devlin every time she'd passed his window and she thought she'd worked out the reason for his suicide attempt. A romantic person herself, she'd imagined a story of unrequited love.

But had he simply tried to run away from a dominant mother?

She worked on in the storeroom for several minutes, until a knock on the door made her turn round. Rob Devlin's visitor was a handsome woman with a kind smile. She was framed in the doorway.

'Are you Bella Denton?'

'Yes, that's right.'

She held out her hand. 'I'm Valerie Blanchard.'

'How do you do?' They shook hands.

'Sister McCrandle told me about what you did for Rob the other day. Raising the alarm, so to speak. I just wanted to pass on my personal thanks.'

'I was just glad I'd been there to help. How is he?'

'Much better. Still in a bit of turmoil but then he always was. Rob is a loner. The kind of boy who's problems tend to overwhelm him - he broods on his own too much.'

'Did he say why he tried to...?'

'Not in so many words, Bella. His mind is still very confused about it all.'

'Has he ever done anything like this before?'

'No, he hasn't,' she said. 'He did once sit on a roof all night in the pouring rain, but that's not quite the same thing is it?'

'Why did he do that?'

'Because the other boys teased him.'

'How many sons do you have?'

Valerie Blanchard laughed. 'None! I'm not married. No, Bella,' she said, 'I was his surrogate mother. I head up a Children's Home. When Rob was with us, I was a house-mother and he was one of my many children.'

Bella gulped. 'You mean, he has no parents?'

'No one he's in touch with. That's part of his problem, I'm afraid. Lack of identity. The feeling that he just doesn't fit in anywhere. It all got much worse after Rob left us.'

'Why, Mrs Blanchard? What happened?'

'Nothing. Nothing at all.' She glanced back at the ward. 'Rob felt completely and utterly rejected. As if nobody in the world cared about him.'

'I do,' said Bella.

'Tell him. Come on. Hearing that is probably the best tonic he can have.'

'But I'm not allowed in the unit.'

'I am - and you're with me. Nobody's going to stop us.'

She led the way purposefully into the Critical Care Unit. Rob was alone, propped up in bed. He looked at them in surprise. After watching him through the window so much, Bella was pleased to meet him face-to-face. But he looked rather defensive.

'This is Bella,' said Valerie Blanchard. 'She wouldn't let me leave until I'd introduced you.'

'Oh?' he said. 'Hi, Bella.'

'Hello. I feel as if I know you already.'

'You seem young to be a nurse.'

'I'm only a student. I've still got a lot to learn.'

'I'm not so sure about that,' said Valerie Blanchard. 'I must have a word with Sister McCrandle. Why don't you keep Rob company until I come back, Bella?'

She went out before either of them could say anything. There was a momentary embarrassment on both sides. Rob was tongue-tied in the presence of such an attractive girl and Bella was still unsure if she ought to be in the unit. She decided to make the most of her brief opportunity.

'Don't do it again, will you?' she said, softly.

He understood what she meant and smiled, self-consciously.

'I'd miss you,' said Bella.

'You would?'

'Of course. So would Mrs Blanchard. Didn't you stop to think how upset she'd be if you had killed yourself?'

'I wasn't sure she'd even remember me.'

'She remembers you all right,' said Bella with a grin. 'How many other boys spent a whole night on the roof in the pouring rain?'

He smiled. 'Did she tell you about that?'

'Yes. You must have got soaked to the skin.'

'I did. I nearly caught pneumonia.'

'But it never happened again.'

'No, Bella. It wasn't a good experience.'

She moved closer to put a hand on his arm.

'Has being in here taught you anything?'

'Look, just leave me alone, will you? I'm still trying to work it out. It's a bit difficult. Being brought back the way I was. I've got to start all over again.' He couldn't help the note of bitterness and hate creeping into his voice.

'With a fresh slate it might make it easier.'

He sighed. 'I don't know about that.'

'What did you do, Rob?'

'Do?'

'Yes. Before you came in here. What sort of job?'

171

'I didn't have one,' he said. 'Nobody would take me on. It was partly my own fault, I suppose. I got very angry because I couldn't find a job. So every time I got an interview, I made a mess of it and rebelled.'

'So what did you do?'

'I drifted. I had this crummy bedsit till the money ran out. Then I started to sleep rough. In shop doorways and things.' He shivered. 'It wasn't too bad in the summer but it was hell when it got cold. Far worse than being on that roof in the rain. I was like some animal curled up in the street. That's when I started thinking about...what I did. Nowhere to go, nothing to do. If I put an end to it all, who'd bother? I was desperate, and I hated everybody. Who would want to care about *me*, anyway?'

'Mrs Blanchard would,' she said, firmly. 'And now I know you a little, I would as well.'

'Why?'

'I just feel involved with you now; don't you care about people when you get involved with them? You won't get rid of me that easily!'

He smiled for the first time. She smiled back so warmly that he saw she really did care. It was a start.

CHAPTER SEVENTEEN

Karlene walked back down the stairs with Janie.

'How did it go?' asked Karlene.

'Not as bad as I thought.'

'He was so happy to see you, Janie.'

'I'm glad I came. It was a bit strange at first but that soon wore off. We had a really good chat.'

Karlene was surprised. 'Vance could actually speak?'

'Sort of. If I put my ear close to his mouth, I could hear what he was trying to say.'

'His diction should get better each time you come.'

'That'll be every day from now on.'

As they crossed Reception, Karlene glanced across at the desk. Harriet was talked about so much in their household that she wanted a closer look at her. She was out of luck. The receptionist was obscured by a tall young doctor. The two were in animated discussion.

'When do you go back to school, Janie?'

'Monday!' she said. 'I'm dreading it, Karlene. After all that's happened. The other kids are bound to pester me with questions. It'll be awful.'

'At least it'll give you chance to see Alex.'

'I'm not sure I want to.'

'What do you mean?'

'Since I lost my Dad, I need Alex more than ever. But if he's gone off me, it could be embarrassing.'

'Stop fearing the worst all the time,' advised Karlene. 'Boys are like that. Make allowances for him. Have faith.'

They came out through the main entrance and paused.

'I can't thank you enough, you've been brilliant, Karlene.'

'I haven't finished yet, Janie. I've got to have a go at that landlord of yours first. I'm seeing the solicitor today with all the evidence I've collected. Bernard Yates won't know what's hit him. That wiring in your house was faulty.'

'Yes,' said Janie. 'That was one of the things Vance told me. He'd seen sparks coming from the socket in the kitchen when he switched on the toaster.' She sighed. 'Not that it matters. Mr Yates'll get out of it somehow.'

'No, he won't,' affirmed Karlene. 'Not if I can help it. He's responsible for the safety of his property. He should've employed a proper electrician to do that work at your house. Not a cowboy. All the tenants I've spoken to are prepared to give evidence about how he's treated them; how he hasn't fulfilled his responsibilities. We're going to succeed, Janie. We won't let your father's death be in vain.'

Janie started to thank her again but Karlene wasn't listening. She was looking towards the main gate over the girl's shoulder. A pale, thin boy in jeans was loitering beside the barrier to the car park. He was looking in their direction.

'I think you've got company, Janie.'

The girl swung round. The boy at the gate waved.

'It's Alex!'

Karlene grinned. 'What are you waiting for!'

———————⋀———————

'Why on earth didn't you do that in the first place, Bel?'

'You didn't ask me.'

'I didn't dare,' said Gordy. 'I thought you'd laugh.'

'I would've.'

'It worked out,' said Mark. 'That's the main thing.'

Gordy chuckled. 'Bel was marvellous. We couldn't have done it better if we'd rehearsed it for a week. Poor old Harriet was gob-smacked. Thanks a million, Bel.'

'It was my way of saying sorry. For yesterday.'

The three friends were lunching together in the canteen. Gordy was basking in his new-found sense of freedom while the student nurses were still enjoying their stint in Marlborough Ward. Mark was pleased that peace had been restored. Now he could stop feeling like a referee.

'We finally found out who Mr Devlin was,' he said.

'Who?' asked Gordy.

'He was brought up in a children's home, and by foster parents. His old house-mother turned

175

up.'

'Yes,' added Bella. 'Valerie Blanchard. She's a nice lady. She thought she knew why he'd jumped from that train.'

'He hadn't bought a ticket.'

'Gordy!'

'Sorry - go on, Bel. Tell me.'

'He's got no family or friends, no job, no money,' she said. 'His future looked so bleak. He felt he had nothing to live for.'

'Rob might think differently now,' said Mark.

'Thanks to Valerie Blanchard,' added Bella. 'She talked to him for ages; she made him feel so much better.'

'You did your bit as well, Bella. I saw you talking with him. I don't know what you said but it certainly cheered him up.'

Mark grinned. 'Wait till he sees your message.'

'Will Sister McCrandle leave it up, though? I put it on the window of the Critical Care Unit.'

Before he could ask her what it was, Gordy was distracted by a grim vision. Harriet was weaving her way towards him through the tables.

'Kiss me again, Bel!' he begged. 'She's back.'

'Could I have a private word, Gordy?' said Harriet.

'I'm rather busy at the moment,' he replied, slipping an arm round Bella and pulling her close. 'As you see.'

'What I see is Bella Denton. And she's not really your girlfriend so you can stop pretending.'

Harriet was in a forceful mood. 'Now, will you come outside, please?'

Gordy made a face but got up and went with her. She led him out to a quiet corner in the corridor and turned to face him.

'It's over,' she said, bluntly.

'What is?'

'You and me, Gordy. Us.'

His heart lifted. 'You mean it?'

'I was having doubts even before that friend of yours kissed you in front of me. That's why I was trying to pin you down to an engagement. For safety reasons.'

'Your safety or mine?'

'Mine, Gordy. I...found my interest was wandering.'

'Harriet!' he said with mock outrage.

'I shouldn't have, I know,' she admitted, 'but he spoke to me every time he went through Reception and...well, I got to like him a lot. He grew on me.'

'Who did?'

'Doctor Holt.'

'Damian?'

'He told me who Bella was,' she explained. 'He saw her rush up and kiss you in Reception. That decided me. You wanted your freedom - I wanted Damian.'

Gordy was peeved. He was happy to get rid of his old flame but he didn't like the feeling of being dumped. That hurt his pride.

'I didn't know you fancied Damian Holt.'

'He looks great in that white coat.'

'House-painters and lab technicians wear those!'

'But Damian is a real doctor.'

'So will I be one day.'

She gave him a farewell peck on his reddening cheek.

'Six years was too long to wait. Goodbye, Gordy.'

───────────⋀───────────

The medication made Rob Devlin sleep for a few hours. When he woke up, he found Gilbert Buchanan examining him. The surgeon was more than satisfied with his patient's progress.

'You're on the mend, Mr Devlin.'

'Am I?'

'As long as you let nature take its course.'

'Will I ever be able to walk properly again?'

'Of course,' said the surgeon. 'Walk, skip, dance. When the plaster finally comes off, you'll be able to enter the London Marathon.'

'When will that be?'

'Oh, you've a long way to go yet. But we won't keep you in here indefinitely. You'll soon be off the critical list.'

'Where will I go then?'

'Into Marlborough Ward. You'll like it there. There will be people you can talk to, counsellors who may be able to help you with your problems.

And you'll have some company, for a start,' said the surgeon. 'It gets very boring being on your own for any length of time. Oh, and you'll be able to meet your friend.'

'What friend?'

'The young lady who sent you that message.'

'I don't know about any message,' said Rob.

'Haven't you seen it?' Gilbert Buchanan chuckled. 'How could you when I've been hovering over you.' He stood out of the way. 'There on the window. Can you read it?'

Bella's message was scrawled on a large piece of white card. She sellotaped it to the outside of the observation window. The patient could read it clearly.

SOMEBODY CARES.

By way of signature, Bella had drawn a nurse's hat.

Rob couldn't help but smile. Bella's drawing looked quite childlike. There were still a lot of problems to be worked through with the psychiatrist in charge of his case but part of his recovery lay in the two words stuck to the window. He'd only met her once but Bella's vitality and directness had boosted his confidence. Somebody really cared about him.

Karlene brought in three mugs of tea from the kitchen.

'Help yourselves,' she said, putting them down.

'Thanks,' said Janie.

'Yeah,' added Alex. 'Thanks.'

'Have you got everything sorted out now, Janie?'

'More or less. It was all a misunderstanding.'

Karlene sighed. 'It usually is.'

After spending the afternoon alone together, the two of them came back to the house for tea with Karlene. They were in an excited mood. Janie had recaptured a little of her vivacity and Alex had a grin on his face.

Karlene liked him. He had a cheeky face and lively blue eyes. He and Janie kept using each other's names and touching each other whenever they could.

'So where did you disappear to, Alex?' said Karlene.

'I thought I'd be in the way.'

'But I needed you, Alex.'

'I know, Janie. And I came round a couple of times. But you were always with someone else. I thought I'd be in the way at a time like that. I couldn't get near you.'

'I thought you'd lost interest.'

'No way! I just...faded into the background.'

'What did I tell you?' said Karlene. 'Have faith.'

'We've had so much to catch up on.'

'Yeah,' said Alex. 'Haven't seen each other for days.'

'Alex sneaked off school to find me,' said Janie.

'You're leading him astray,' teased Karlene. 'So what's the next step? Are you hoping to carry on as before?'

''Course,' said Alex.

'Why not?' added Janie.

'Because there might be a much easier way.'

Janie and Alex looked at each other in bewilderment.

'You love each other, don't you?' said Karlene.

'Yes!' said Janie. 'Don't we, Alex?'

He grinned and nodded. His wavy hair shook.

'Then why keep hiding it away?'

'We've got to, Karlene,' he said. 'There's Janie's family, for a start. They'd never accept me. Then there's my parents. They're funny about these things.'

'Most people are,' observed Karlene.

'It's much better to keep it secret,' argued Janie.

'But it isn't. You've just proved that. As soon as there's a crisis, you completely flip. You think Alex has deserted you and he believes he's only in the way.'

'We've got no choice, Karlene.'

'Yes, you have. You're not like Vance.'

'Vance?'

'He really doesn't have any choice,' she

explained. 'That fire has scarred his face for life. No matter how good the plastic surgery, he'll go out into the world knowing he looks a bit abnormal. Everyone will stare at first. Vance will have to handle that for the rest of his life.'

'What's that got to do with us?' said Alex.

'He'll be like you two. Ashamed to be seen.'

'We're not ashamed!' denied Janie, hotly.

'It's just not possible,' said Alex. 'There'd be a riot.'

'For a time, maybe. But people would soon get used to it. As they'll get used to Vance. He's got real disfigurement to worry about. Think how brave he needs to be. All you're hiding is love.'

They held hands and looked at each other again.

'Besides,' said Karlene with a mischievous grin, 'it would be worth it, wouldn't it?'

'Yeah!' said Alex with enthusiasm.

'I'm not sure,' said Janie. 'I have to think of Mum.'

'Oh, come on!' chided Karlene. 'If you'd always put your mother first, this friendship with Alex would never have got off the ground. You like each other, so have the courage to come out and say so.' She shrugged. 'I did.'

'You?' said Alex.

'I had a white boyfriend at school. Carlo. Well, he was Italian, actually. His parents ran a fish and chip shop. He was a real laugh.'

Janie was fascinated. 'What happened?'

'What you'd expect. His parents complained, my parents complained, the other kids teased us rotten for a while.'

'And then?'

'They accepted it,' said Karlene. 'In fact, when we finally broke up, my mother burst into tears. She'd really got to like him. She told me off for giving him the elbow.'

The two of them thought about this. They sipped their tea.

'It's a big step,' said Alex.

'You'll have to take it sooner or later.'

'She's right, Alex.'

'Janie needs help and support. You can't give her that if you only meet in secret at certain times.'

'That's true. This needs thinking about.'

A key turned in the lock. Janie and Alex jumped.

'Relax,' said Karlene. 'It's only my friends.'

'But they'll see us!' said Janie.

'It won't matter.'

Mark and Suzie came into the room. Karlene waved her hand.

'Suzie and Mark meet Janie and Alex.'

'Hi,' said Suzie, pleasantly.

'Nice to meet you,' said Mark. 'You'll have to excuse us, Karlene. We're going to the pool.'

'Bye, Janie,' said Suzie. 'Bye, Alex.'

She and Mark went upstairs to collect their towels and swimming costumes. Janie and Alex relaxed slightly.

'You got over that first hurdle pretty well,' said Karlene. 'They didn't turn a hair. I'm black but none of my friends mind sharing the house with me. Until I hog the bathroom, that is. We all get on fine together. As you saw.'

She turned to Janie. 'I've got some good news for you. From that solicitor I saw today. He was very impressed with all the evidence I'd got about Bernard Yates. I even got a copy of the official report on the cause of the fire. The solicitor said we had your landlord over a barrel. You definitely will get compensation. We're going to get that guy who caused you to lose your home and your dad's death.'

Janie's face glowed.

'Why not go straight home and pass on the good tidings to your mother? Then - while she's in a good mood - introduce Alex.'

'That's not such a bad idea, Janie,' he said.

Janie nodded enthusiastically. She finished her cup of tea and got up. They said their goodbyes and Karlene showed them out. They had arrived separately. They left together.

Karlene took the cups into the kitchen. Suzie and Mark came racing happily down the stairs with their swimming gear.

'Why not come with us, Karlene?' said Mark.

'I'm too tired.'

'Float on top of the water.'

'I'd sink like a stone.'

They heard someone else let themselves in.

Gordy came into the living room with his arm round Bella.

'That's better!' said Suzie with approval.

'We're the best of friends now,' said Bella.

'It's been a wonderful day,' said Gordy. 'I finally got Harriet off my back.'

'I had my first go with an X-ray machine,' said Suzie.

'I emptied six bedpans,' said Mark.

'I had a great day as well,' decided Bella. 'I made it up with Gordy and got through to Rob at last. That was a big thrill for me. Really being able to help him.'

'What about you, Kar?' said Gordy. 'What did *you* do today?'

'Me?' said Karlene, thinking of the traumas she'd shared with Janie. 'Oh...campaigned against a criminal, did my revision, this and that...all the everyday things students like us usually do!'

Lions

CITY HOSPITAL SERIES
by Keith Miles

Discover City Hospital and the five young recruits who work there. Experience the high drama and the humour of life in a large, modern hospital. Everything from romance to radiotherapy - drama to drudgery, from fun to fatigue. If you can take the pressure, it's all here!

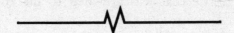

CITY
HOSPITAL

NEW BLOOD

As soon as the ambulance stopped, its doors opened and the stretcher was lifted swiftly but gently to the ground. The small boy with the chubby face lay pale and motionless on his back. As one of the paramedics wheeled him into Casualty, another walked alongside, holding the plastic bottle that was attached to his arm by a tube.

Dr Damian Holt was waiting with a nurse in a bay that was curtained off by a plastic sheet. One look at the patient told him that the boy was in a critical condition.

Two lives hang in the balance at City Hospital - but Suzie's involvement in the first means her life is in danger too.

CITY HOSPITAL

FEVER

Bella was stunned. 'Mrs Elliott isn't *dead* is she?'

'Yes, I'm afraid so. We did all we could but...'
Her voice trailed off - she looked shocked and
confused herself.

'What was the cause of death?'

Sister Morgan's face changed. Bella had never
seen her look like that before; a look of fear and
bewilderment. It was as if she'd come up against
something completely outside her experience. It
scared her. She bit her lip and shook her head
sadly.

'We don't know, Bella,' she admitted. 'We
just don't know.'

Feelings run to fever-pitch at City Hospital - will
someone crack under the strain?

CITY
HOSPITAL

EMERGENCY

'Out!' repeated Jez. 'Or she gets it!'

Two more security guards had arrived and were looking in through the window. They watched as their colleague slowly backed out of the office with the two male nurses. Jez Halliday held the advantage for the moment and there was little that they could do. Sister Poole and Bella Denton were hostages.

'Stay back!' he yelled. 'Or I blow her brains out!'

A high-tension hostage situation puts the whole of City Hospital on edge – who will break the deadlock?

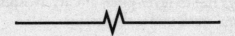